OPEN ME

a novel by
Sunshine O'Donnell

OPEN ME

a novel by
Sunshine O'Donnell

MACADAM CAGE

MacAdam Cage
155 Sansome Street, Suite 150
San Francisco, CA 94104
www.MacAdamCage.com

Library of Congress Cataloging-in-Publication Data

O'Donnell, Sunshine.
  Open me : a novel / by Sunshine O'Donnell.
    p. cm.
  ISBN 978-1-59692-204-4 (alk. paper)
  1. Weepers (Mourners)--Fiction. 2. Girls--Fiction. I. Title.
PS3615.D66O64 2007
813'.6--dc22

                                    2006103281

Paperback edition: June 2007
ISBN 978-1-59692-236-5

Book and cover design by Dorothy Carico Smith
Printed in the United States of America
1 2 3 4 5 6 7 8 9 0

For my family

A secret is an outside that is inside,
a secretion is an inside that is outside.
—Mark C. Taylor, Tears

In 1999, a seventeen-year-old girl from suburban Philadelphia was the last person in the United States to be arrested for being paid to cry at funerals. The officers who charged her never knew her real name. In all of the reports available, she is referred to only as *Mirabelle, Wailer.*

It wasn't until Mirabelle's arrest was published in newspapers that local residents understood that this little-known and dying art, called *Wailing*, had managed to survive as an underground profession in some parts of North America. For thousands of years, wealthy families around the world have paid Wailers, Weeping Maids, and Wailing Women to perform at burials, a tradition still employed by contemporary funeral directors when there are too few mourners in attendance during burials, or when surviving relatives feel the need to have someone else "translate their grief" for them.

The controversial training techniques used to coach young would-be Wailers (emotional abuse, abandonment, the forced fondling of corpses) have been grounds for twenty-six states to pass legislation banning professional mourning, though most of these laws had never been enforced until Mirabelle's performances were featured in a local newspaper article in 1987. The strictest of these prohibitions was passed in Mirabelle's home state of Pennsylvania before the turn of the century. Today, there are fewer than ten apprenticing professional mourners still working in America, many living in states where new Wailing prohibitions are being strongly enforced by police.

According to legend, Mirabelle's gift for crying on cue came to her when she was six years old, working a Bucks County funeral with her mother and aunt in 1985. Between 1985 and 1999, funeral directors throughout the tri-state area hired Mirabelle and her late mother hundreds of times through contracts with set fees. Mirabelle quickly became known throughout the East Coast's death industry as the most successful professional mourner of her generation, a title rivaled only by the fame of her own mother. By the time she was arrested in 1999, Mirabelle had worked thousands of high-end funerals, including several celebrity interments, and was estimated to be worth roughly half a million dollars.

Today, Mirabelle is in her twenties, although—as there is no legal documentation of her birth, life, or education—there is no way to confirm her actual age. Mirabelle continues to refuse to speak to the press and does not allow photographs. Those who have seen her in person as an adult report that she is still quite small, barely five feet tall, with a chalk white complexion, waist-length black hair, and a narrow, child-like build.

Because it is forbidden for a Wailer to reveal details of her apprenticeship, career, or ancestral history, under pain of exclusion and the disgrace of her bloodline, no one has encountered a complete first-hand account as of yet. Luckily, a few dozen historical fragments related to wailing have been discovered, some including trade secrets that have been passed down from mother to daughter for more than six thousand years.

TABLE OF CONTENTS

TABLE OF CONTENTS – HISTORICAL ARTIFACTS

1

"Do you know what you look like when you're crying?"

The little girl and the old man who paid for her are standing beneath the deep green grave canopy when he asks her this. It's the same question she is asked by most people, along with a battery of other questions she will never be allowed to answer. *Is it true your mother tortured you to teach you how to cry? Is it true you worship goddesses and never went to school? Do you know that it's illegal? How much money do you make?*

The little girl does not answer any of the man's questions. They stand on opposite sides of the casket, waiting for its slow drop to end so that the little girl can begin. While they wait, the little girl picks at the edges of her handkerchief and watches the sleek brown coffin that is dropping, the shrinking gap between the casket and the hole, while her mother stands behind the real mourners, counting the money and turning away.

On top of the canopy, big drops of rain fall like a sky-full of beads shaken out of a sheet. The little girl listens to them burst against the taut canvas tent and knows that the rain wouldn't taste like tears, it would taste like metal and freshly dug dirt. She imagines this taste, wishes she could sit in the playroom at home and watch the silvery buds cling to the storm windows as they grow and loosen their grip, melt into each other and desperately roll. They still call it a *playroom*, even though she is now a star without much time to play. Instead of toys, the small room is crammed with pieces of furniture that need to be fixed: a cracked plastic sewing table, her Aunt Ayin's mirror, exhausted-looking cardboard boxes. A heavy cream curtain, its edges scalloped with rust-colored stains, hangs against one wall to hide the hot-water heater.

"Come a bit closer for me," says the old man, gently. "A bit closer to the grave."

Is the young minister still talking? The little girl can't tell, can't hear much but the sound of her stiff black lace rustling against itself, the rain, the sound of her heart in her ears. She knows what she's supposed to do and how to do it. She's been training at it for years. It's what she does best, better than anyone, better even than her own mother. At least that's what the widows say: *A professional, a lady, a legend, a star.* She tries to be sad but she doesn't feel sad now. What she feels inside is the ghost-self growing, curled at the edges, gray and unstable as burnt paper. A scorched wisp.

She moves closer to the grave. *I am stupid,* she remembers. *I am worthless, I am disgusting.* The grass by her feet is fake and bright green, fringed with frail shards of gnarled brown leaves. Of all the months, the girl likes the smell of October best, even better when wet, she loves to watch her feet walk through the leaves and their just-before-dying smell. In her townhouse development, the October air carries smells the way cloth does, it touches her and is gone, a flash of dead leaves, fabric softener from the dryer vents, rain, exhaust fumes, fire. Today the wet chill doesn't cling to her, though the leaves are wet and cling to her shiny black shoes like little drowned men. By November the smell will be gone. It will get dark and cold and it will stay dark and cold for a very long time.

She can feel the old man staring. She knows what she looks like, the white face, the famous black dress, and she feels dulled by a veil of dust. When she was younger the newspapers had called her *gaunt,* but this was because of an old Wailers' trick, putting a thin girl in a thick dress too large and long for her frame. Now she feels as if she is wearing a flesh suit instead of a body. Behind the long hair, the little girl's face looks scared.

"Don't be scared," the old man says and, with some difficulty, he walks closer to where she is and stands behind her, clamping his hands down onto the shoulders of her dress. His fingers shake as he leans forward, whispering into the little girl's hair.

What does he whisper? At first she can't tell, the rain is beating its glass fists against the tent. She closes her eyes and pretends she's under her secret salt tree with leaves like thin tongues of glass. The old man's fingers press and squeeze. She thinks he says, *Look at yourself, aren't you lovely?* She keeps trying but the tears won't come, she only sees white, white on white, something she can barely see the shape of, like a reflection caught in a puddle of milk. She doesn't want to leave the salt tree but it is too late, the man's whispers reach her even there, his not-white sounds, his wordless noises navigating toward her through the salt wasps and dry flowers.

What does he whisper? *Unbearable.* A hot breath, damp and loose. *Unbearable.* A wet smoke.

If you don't cry for me I will turn your mother in.

She opens her eyes and looks at her hands and sees the color gray. The little girl feels his fingers squeeze, his breath get thick, his dank gray whisper. The ghost inside her is whisper thin. The old man doesn't know her name. He whispers, gently, into her hair, *Start crying.*

— 1922 A.D., LONDON, ENGLAND —
Author Unknown

THE OBSCENE ARTS:
MATERIALS TOWARDS A HISTORY OF WAILING WOMEN
and Other Professional Mourners
1922
PART III.
TRAINING THE NOVICE.—*Continued.*

D. METHODS OF ABUSE.

On The Importance of Self-Loathing

Used properly, the silent repetition of humiliating comments about oneself is often the most practical method a novice can implement in order to arouse sudden weeping. For instance, the traditional prompts *I am stupid, I am worthless, I am disgusting*, have been indispensable for generations of professional mourners who would otherwise have found themselves dry at graveside and thus unable to perform for their wage. Be warned that this technique must be handled with great skill and delicacy, as it can be dangerously mismanaged by the naïve and may result in suicide or the permanent disordering of the brains.

On this point should be mentioned the value of a mother's role in the fabrication, penetration, and reinforcement of such statements which, although seemingly painful to absorb, will ultimately serve the novice once they are remembered at appropriate times (e.g. at gravesides or while procuring contracts). Some suggestions include disturbing comments concerning the girl's intelligence, talent, worth, and virtue. It has been proven

unwise, however, to berate a novice about her appearance, as a girl's confidence about her ability to charm will play a critical role in the acquisition
of new clients throughout her life.

If, by the time the novice has completed her apprenticeship, she is still
unable to discern between her true feelings of self-worth and the poor
esteem she must draw upon while coaxing tears from her eyes, she will
eventually find herself unhinged and perpetually weeping without cause.
To avoid this most appalling condition, a mother must determine whether
her daughter is of an especially weak or inconsolable constitution before
beginning a regimen of verbal assaults. However, if it becomes clear that
the novice will be unable to perform without abuse, by all means employ
whatever practices are necessary. Although not ideal, it is, after all, more
profitable to have a daughter who weeps all of the time than one who must
be abandoned because she cannot weep at all.

2

"Is it true you worship goddesses and never went to school?"

Mem was six years old when she was finally allowed to see her First Corpse. It was something she had looked forward to for a long time, although she didn't like the sound of the word *corpse*. She loved, instead, the word *deceased*. It sounded like the first few seconds of water surging from a faucet, or the beginning of a song, although her kind didn't know many songs, they weren't allowed to listen to the radio or watch television. Mem was not supposed to want to have anything to do with the outside world, and she wasn't supposed to desire things. She had been taught that the things she touched or thought she owned—like the new metal swing-set in the backyard, the bright stack of *Letter People* books (*Mr. P with a Purple Pillow, Mr. M with a Munching Mouth*), the wall-to-wall confetti-colored carpet under her feet—would exist long after her body had liquefied, and then even those things would not survive the next flood, asteroid, or ice age. The slow burn of oxygen would chew chemicals and atoms to smaller bits and then these would also be pried apart, revealing something even smaller but just as fragmented and temporary. To the unprofessionals, tangible things seemed to promise immortality, proof, a permanent record, but even as a little girl Mem knew that *permanent* was a fairy-tale word. Like *the end*. Or *forever*.

Of course this never stopped Mem from wanting things. When she

and her cousin Sofie were very small and just starting their apprentice-
ships, all Mem wanted was a pink dress frothy as a whipped dessert, a grit-
filled Big Wheel, a dog, a cadre of friends who wore Band-Aids like
badges. Mem and Sofie sat at the tile-topped table in Mem's mother's
kitchen, swinging their legs under the chairs as they shared a packet of but-
terscotch Krimpets. *Here is the first Lesson, and the first secret you must keep.*
They nodded, dreaming of dogs and dresses, scraped the icing off the plastic wrappers with their teeth.

By the day she saw her First Corpse and worked her First Funeral,
Mem had memorized all of the Lessons. She could recite her maternal
ancestry all the way back to ancient Rome, and she knew every step of her
history. Her favorite part was during their wailing glory, in England, when
the kings sent black cloaks and baskets of berries before each funeral
parade. The Wailers then only ate berries that bled. They needed them to
make their mouths red, a glistening and conspicuous health next to the
powdered pall of their dull white flesh. On the streets, at their cue, two
thousand mourners would wail as they stumbled and caterwauled through
the cobblestone streets. Their wigs fell off, they moaned in grief.
Emotional decadence! Voluptuous suffering! A carnival of exquisite woe! The
others stood to the side, breathless, holding their applause.

Before this was Rome and the sprigs of rosemary they'd sewn, like
brides, into the tightly tucked hems of their shifts. There they howled over
fresh graves and snapped their own finger joints like asparagus tips. There
once were white saris and platters of salt, then togas with bloodstains and
garlands of thorns. On the islands they tore through their ear lobes,
knocked out their teeth, and poisoned the dogs. They chanted and carved
their own scalps with shells, their unbridled and nut-brown breasts swinging with each slice.

The unprofessionals said *Savage orgies. Decrepit display. Ostentatious
grief.*

As always there were flowers.

Mem loved learning her history but what she was made to learn best
was that she had been born, like all of the women before her, to become a

star. She would easily have sacrificed all of the other things she thought she wanted in order to become a legend like her mother. Each day Mem watched her mother prepare for work, painting her face and buttoning her doole, the traditional black dress hand-made for mourning. Mem could not wait for the day when she too would have those long black coils of glossy hair, the deep green eyes, and breasts so big she would have to lift them up to wash underneath. While Mem's mother and Aunt Ayin, Sofie's mother, sat at the table and taught the girls their Lessons, Mem would look at her mother and feel her heart crack open with love. Mem's mother was tall and broad, an unbroken surface, heavily outlined and magically back-lit by light like the paintings of saints. Her bones were strong. Her mouth was lush. She was powerful enough for herself and Mem and all the space in between. She was massive but compact, a spoonful of dead star that no one else could lift. Mem looked at her mother, the wide red lips and blue-black hair oiled into snakes, and inside of Mem's chest thrilled a love that whirled in a small hurricane. "These are the Lessons our kind has been handing down for six thousand years," Mem's mother said to the girls. "You may never reveal the Lessons to the unprofessionals, no matter how much they might beg you."

Mem cannot remember how old she was when she first realized that she was part of a *kind*. Until they were older, Mem and Sofie thought that playing Funeral was something all children did. They watched the other children who lived in Mem's townhouse development come home from their schools and play their games, and during these games someone always died. The players argued endlessly about whose turn it was to stagger and moan, then fall and slump to the ground. But all of these pretend deaths were temporary, and none of them went so far as to be mourned. When Sofie and Mem played and argued about whose turn it was to die, they were playing legendary Wailers, and corpses who were already dead.

Mem's favorite game was called *Open Me*. One player pretended to be their legendary great-grandmother, whose public name was Ruth, and the other pretended to be the undertaker who split open her belly and found a lifetime of treasures hidden inside. *Open me* was what the famous letter had said, the one that Ruth left on the bed-stand for her daughters to find when she died. It was a sacrilegious request, but it was a last request nonetheless, and one particularly fitting to Ruth's history. As a baby, Ruth had been cut out of a deceased mother who was unearthed from her casket when a servant heard moaning coming from the freshly-interred grave. The infant Ruth survived this ordeal, grew to be a beautiful woman, bore seven girls of her own, and became the most celebrated Wailer in Italy before she was forty years old.

But the peculiar theme of premature burial stayed with Ruth throughout her life. During her professional prime, premature burial had become so common that preventative handbooks were distributed all over Europe, and each year new techniques and detection-devices were created to better ascertain just how dead a body really was. It was not unusual to see caskets being dug up while services were performed across the way. As a result, hundreds of exhumed bodies were discovered to have been buried alive, most found face-down in their caskets with broken fingers, deep teeth-marks sunk into shoulders and arms, and winding sheets shredded and soaked through with fluids.

When Ruth was a young mother, a gang of Ressurectionists stole one of her clients' corpse just hours after he was buried and sold it to local doctors for educational dissection. After the first small incision had been made in his chest, the man sat up on the table, mumbled something, and swooned. When he woke the next morning he explained that what he had been trying to say was *I am not dead*. He described how he had listened, in horror, as his family discussed burial plans, and later how he had heard his small son clapping with glee at the prospect of inheriting his horse.

Because these dark mistakes occurred frequently, Ruth was often well paid to wail twice for the same man, and she soon earned enough to bring her children to Philadelphia. She lost two girls to cholera during the boat trip, but she had deliberately given birth to many daughters in the hope that at least a few might survive to adulthood and fame.

Once in America, Ruth adored two sets of things: her beautiful wailing daughters and her silver, the first set anyone in her family had ever earned. She lavished her girls with silk mourning gowns and polished the silver herself once a week. When Ruth suddenly died at the age of eighty-six, she was found fully dressed in her bed, holding two dozen gleaming spoons against her chest with both hands like a bridal bouquet. Next to her body she had left a note, with two words written in her well-schooled calligraphy: *Open me.*

Before the opening, the undertaker was surprised to find Ruth's stomach unnaturally lumpy and enlarged. He carefully prodded and poked from the outside, then slit the organ open. Inside he discovered a hoard of things that Ruth had managed to swallow. The small spoons, brooches, brass keys, and bracelets were removed and boiled and then given to Mem's grandmother, who later sold most of the cache during the Great Depression. Mem's mother inherited one of the bracelets. It hangs above the mantel in Mem's house, behind glass, with the clasp part tacked down, one of the few artifacts left from six thousand years of ancestry. Three of the milky white beads dangle from the bottom like loose teeth. When Mem was little she would look longingly at the bracelet, knowing that someday it would be hers. She couldn't wait to remove it from the glass and wear it, she wouldn't care if it broke. This is what *things* were meant for, she had learned, to be used until they fell to pieces.

"As an apprentice just starting, you must model yourself after Aurora, Roman goddess of the dawn who every day wakes to weep morning dew," her mother explained in her deep, steady voice. "Aurora was the first Wailer, from which we all came, and she still works every day, all over the planet, waking each morning to remember her murdered son and then cry on cue. As always her veils are deepest black. And as always there are flowers."

Mem was convinced that one day she would look up and see Aurora, working above the telephone poles and static billboard smiles outside of Mem's suburban development, riding the dawn like a chariot while the sky yawned its new sun and crept after her with puddles of light. Aurora would shed her veils and unpin her doole, dropping layers and ribbons and plumes of gray that would hang suspended over Mem's yellow townhouse like the ghosts of clothes. Aurora's tears were so fine you couldn't catch them in a bottle, though once Mem and Sofie actually tried, standing toe-deep in new sod and pebbles, foolishly holding an empty cup open to a sky that had already passed them by.

"She is such a good Wailer she can even make the houses cry, look!" Mem's mother said. She pointed to dewdrops dripping down the storm windows while Mem and Sofie stood on tiptoe, watching the rivulets gather and streak down the glass. The windowpanes flashed in the loud morning sun and to Mem they cried like astonished eyes.

On that day Mem's mother was so beautiful she was like a bright light that hurt to look at.

On that day she was the youngest she would ever be.

Mem's mother had turned to the girls and placed a strong hand on the top of each of their heads. She said, "What you are learning is the language of water. Even in this culture of toilets and forecasters and containment, nothing else on Earth can cleanse or destroy like water. Every tear we're paid to shed still possesses this cathartic and catastrophic power, and the clients know this. For them our tears are not water but analgesic, aphrodisiac, intoxicant, poison. Crying is a three-dimensional language, a language that tells a story one can touch as well as see, a native tongue that all children know as they gasp their way out of the womb. It is a true language that survives evolution, technology, and time. It is the only language that survives translation."

It would be a long time before Mem understood this, but she didn't mind being confused. Her mother's hand on her head was a blessing, a shield, it sent waves of love into Mem's marrow. She didn't know, then, that this love was a six-thousand-year-old tradition, too, a link from mother to daughter that could not be explained to someone who did not already understand. It was already the unspoken part of her training, this sense that without her mother, Mem would be nothing. And the knowledge that if Mem could not, would not perform well, her mother would have to leave her behind.

Next to the stack of old copies of *American Funeral Monthly* on the end of the table, Mem's mother had piled several of her meticulous charts, diagrams of the deceased, careful family trees of as many of her clients as she could document. At night Mem would watch her mother pour over these charts while her tea got cold, rubbing her heels together, whispering things to herself about first-born deaths, making shorthand marks next to each name. This was Mem's mother's only real involvement with the world of the unprofessionals, although when she was younger and did not know any better, Mem's mother had sometimes accepted the widows' invitations to come back to the house where the mourners were gathering. The survivors always watched to make sure that she didn't eat too much or steal anything or strangely continue to weep while everyone else whispered and the children played out back with the dogs as though it was any other day. The adults were always curious at these gatherings; they would watch her, staring at her blacks, asking questions between bites of deviled eggs. *How did you get into such a business?* they would inquire, eyes wide. *Is there some sort of school for this? I thought it was against the law.* They would watch her as if she was from another time and place, an Old West prostitute, a New England witch. As if she might, at any moment, burn the house to the ground in grief or throw herself screaming into a ditch.

In her ancestors' days, these actions might have been appropriate, perhaps even conservative. Mem's mother wanted to look at the mourners' insipid faces and say *We once ate the flesh of corpses beneath fig trees, drove nails through the heads and eyes of the dead, danced around funeral pyres, wore dooles made of the deceased's hair. We strangled their daughters. We scratched their faces to bleeding and dripped our own blood into graves. You know who I am. I'm a star. You paid me because I'm a star.* When Wailers were still allowed to work Jewish funerals, the shiva-goers would stare at Mem's mother as if she might suddenly drop her paper cup of lukewarm coffee and dance around the plastic-covered furniture, chanting. Instead, Mem's mother would politely excuse herself and go back to her car. Check the receipts, take some notes. Jot a few things down on her chart. Busy herself with the business of things, the craft and trade. The profession.

A professional.

A lady.

If Mem's mother stared at the numbers long enough, the churning sensation, the sudden drop and burn in her belly that the questions had provoked, would start to fade, diminishing into a small stain of feeling that was easy to brush into some abandoned corner of herself.

A professional. A lady. A legend. A star. Mem's mother would say these things to herself over and over again, remembering who she was.

The night before her First Funeral, Mem repeats the same words to herself. *A professional. A lady. A legend. A star.* All of the things she would finally be allowed to become. Cool slices of moonlight seam through the gold metal slats of her blinds and she remembers the story Aunt Ayin told them about how the moon was once as bright as the sun. Too bright, according to God, who got irritated and sent the moon a message: *Go and diminish thyself.*

God, said Aunt Ayin, was pissed off. Why was the moon acting this way? Didn't she know that when he created the sun it was supposed to be the most luminous, the most powerful beacon in the heavens? Didn't she know that the Earth needed to have only half a day of light, then half a day of dark?

The moon wouldn't listen. She was stubborn. She lit all her wicks and let them burn. *Diminish thyself? Diminish this*! But God wasn't playing. He sent an army of tempests to put her out. One by one they extinguished her fluted edges of light, leaving behind a complexion of hard pockets and pores. She tried to resist but it was no good, the tempests were too strong. She could feel her flesh callus as they snuffed her out, leaving her chalky and itchy with ash. And what did her sister moons and stars say?

It's better this way. You have to let go. So sorry for your loss.

Mem knows that tomorrow she will prove herself to be a better daughter than the moon was, she will begin her own legend, standing at the grave as her legacy comes up out of her mouth, a beautiful thing growing open and flooding outward, an arching deluge and then the hiss of drips rushing into momentary chandelier crystals from her eyes that will thaw and melt before they hit the ground. She will be like Aurora. She will be like her mother. She will be like all of the women who have come before her, and her mother will not have to leave her.

Mem can't see much out of the window through the slats but she knows that once morning comes, Aurora's legend will take over where the moon's will leave off, her dramatic dew-beads soon swelling and running together, rushing to the tips of leaves and low petals, sulky waters dangling like glass fruits from the loose lips of flowers. They will frost strange shapes on the aluminum siding, make the matted grass stiffen and glisten. Even the scratched Plexiglas 7-Eleven windows around the corner will soon be spangled and slick. When Mem envisions the sadness of the moon, this is what she thinks of: waterlogged windows without anything to shutter them. Eyes wet with someone-else's tears. A borrowed grief. An outside leak.

In bed Mem closes her own eyes and sees spirals of no-color in hot curls of wire, not-red, not-white, not-green, not-brown. The color blue is Aurora in the mornings with vapors falling soft like feathers from her eyes. The color blue is the word *weep* weeping from her lips.

Mem keeps her eyes closed and she sees blue. She sees Aurora wreathed in blue. She sees Aurora tearing at her hair. She sees her plucking at her flesh. She hears her secrets. She hears her sobs.

She hears her waters weeping over Mem's bones.

— 1986 A.D., PENNSYLVANIA, UNITED STATES —
EXCERPT, *Montgo Times*

Mother Abandons Daughter, Neighborhood Baffled
By Staff Writer J.W. Stuart

For the past fifteen weeks, a seven-year-old girl lived alone in an abandoned Glenside row home after she was deserted by her mother. The girl had managed to feed, clean and clothe herself throughout the ordeal, but by the time social service workers located her yesterday she was emaciated and traumatized. The two-month-old corpse of the family dog was found lying in the kitchen, covered in sheets of notebook paper and pages torn from the girl's coloring book.

Over the past two years, three other young Delaware Valley girls have been found deserted in their own homes by their single mothers. City agencies have been unable to locate birth certificates, social security cards, medical documents, school information or extended family members.

Until yesterday, 47-year-old Glenside resident Fiona Paulo-Marnessa had no idea that the mother and daughter who had lived next door for the past twelve years were allegedly embroiled in a bizarre scandal that would soon shock her neighborhood. Marnessa, a mother of three, described the mother as "nice but shy...an overweight, middle-aged woman with short blond hair and...a nice smile."

"I thought the little girl was being home-schooled and they were just a very private family," said Marnessa. "I can't...believe how wrong I was."

Marnessa realized something was amiss last Sunday

when, while planting flowers in her front garden, she watched half a dozen police cars pull into her street. Marnessa recalled that the officers quickly stepped out of their vehicles and began to bang on her neighbor's door. Receiving no response, the door was kicked in and police entered the house.

"I tried to ask them what was going on but no one would tell me," Marnessa said.

About ten minutes later, an officer stepped out of the house with the little girl in his arms just as an ambulance pulled up. The child was wrapped in a blanket, Marnessa recalled, and buckled into a gurney in the back of the ambulance.

Like Marnessa, residents throughout the area were concerned with the morning's events. That afternoon, the precinct in charge of coordinating the operation refused to provide any information regarding the event, citing the case as sensitive. On Monday, Lt. Condenisha Tish told the Times that while it would be unwise to release any official statements before detectives have completed their investigation, it is believed that the girl's mother was a member of a local cult that allegedly requires participants to "force their children to cry at funerals for money and…abandon them if they can't do it."

"It's no secret that the whole [district] has been cracking down on this group," she said. "There aren't many of them…left. They're not a violent group and we've never had a case where…someone outside of the group has been coerced to join. Residents have no real reason to be concerned."

But Marnessa, like many of her neighbors, can't help but be concerned.

"It's like we all live here and this terrible thing

happened right under our noses," she said. "That poor little girl…"CONTINUED J-16

3

"How much money do you make?"

Unlike her mother, Mem never cared about the money. All she want-ed was to be loved. When she became older, anyone who ever watched her work fell a little bit in love with her, at least momentarily, but none of these people really knew anything about her. They never even knew her real name.

"Never disclose your real name to the unprofessionals, no matter how much they might beg you," Mem's mother had said. "Your secret name is powerful and, like all powerful things, can be easily misused. The crude names of the unprofessionals are not hidden because these names are words with no meaning. A Wailer's name is her link to her line, her moth-er, her value, her trade. To know someone's true name is to know her lin-eage. To know someone's true name is to know her destiny."

Mem was the secret name, an ancient word that came from an upside-down tree with roots reaching up to the sky, a head of old fingers stirring the cosmos like soup. The twenty-two paths of a secret alphabet formed this tree and were engraved, like tombstones, into the breath of God. *Mem* was one of the important letters, meaning *of water, of above, of the belly, of salt.*

But the salt Mem's kind spoke of was not the same kind of salt the unprofessionals used to season their taupe, bland food. The salt of Mem's heritage had meaning the same way that all of their secret names had meaning, because without salt there would be no tears. Mem's family line went back to the *Via Salaria*, the Salt Road in Italy, when salt was the greatest commodity of all, and Mem's mother owned several antique salt cellars full of *fleur de sel*, the cream of all salts, a glinting gray snow of salt kept for good luck.

On the day of Mem's First Funeral, she awakes knowing that she will be given a sealed locket full of sacred salt from the *Via Salaria* to wear for good fortune. She will be anointed with olive oil on her temples and finally given her first real doole. She is six years old, and as she waits in the hallway for her mother to finish in the bathroom, Mem pulls at the wooly pills of her footy pajamas, shaking her foot so that she can hear the mysterious crumbs trapped in the toe of the plastic sole. She whispers the word *deceased*. She can hear her mother on the other side, opening and closing jars and sighing to herself, *This is the youngest I will ever be.*

Mem whispers the word *death*, her lips almost touching the bathroom door. She can feel the air from her breath hit the wood veneer and fan out. It doesn't sound like anything, really, a weak, nothing word. A little girl's name. For years Mem has seen scores of the almost-dead in the retirement homes where the mothers do business, urine-scented buildings where people go to become almost nothing, wrinkly dehydrated children or fleshy rubber balloons with hair. While Mem's mother writes receipts and asks questions of surviving spouses, Mem steals glances at the mummified, husk-and-fingernail people and puts them into categories: *Open-mouth breathers. Oozers. Smilers. Cripples. Tubers with inside parts on the outside.* And *Screamers*.

No matter how high-end, the retirement homes the mothers use for contracts smell of unwashed wrinkles, the clinical white corridors lined with robot parts and people in nightclothes and wheelchairs, staring at walls. Whenever Mem steps inside of these places, the old people make great efforts to notice her as she walks by, as if someone has brought them a present, except for the Screamers, who ignore her and shriek unusual things. There was one Screamer, a frail little woman with pink patches of scalp showing through her scant hair, who sat in the courtyard and shrieked, "Help me! Help me!" over and over. The sound was so awful that it did make Mem want to help her. But help her do what? The woman was clean and fully dressed, her spindly legs covered in a homemade afghan, with a male nurse standing right next to her.

"Help me! Oh, help me!" screamed the woman.

Please be quiet, thought Mem.

"Help me!" screamed the woman, her voice cracking.

As if someone was hurting her. As if she was trapped somewhere and couldn't get out.

This is the youngest I will ever be.

On the other side of the bathroom door, Mem is frightened by the sound of her mother's voice. It is unlike her mother to sound so sad and submissive. Mem looks at the photo of her mother on the hallway wall, a studio picture taken before Mem was born, during her mother's professional heyday, with the bold blue backdrop and stiff bubble hairdo that were so stylish then. In the picture Mem's mother is not weeping but she holds a hand-stitched handkerchief like a wilted and decadent flower just beneath a bright red but calm, closed mouth. This is before the brassieres sculpted strap-shaped dips into her olive shoulders and the veins in her hands pushed their way up to the surface like eroded roots. Before things began to ferment, dimpling the smoothness of Mem's mother's legs.

Once, before she was Mem's mother, Mem's mother's charms stuck out like flags sailing the wind and capturing innocent passers-by. As she walked to gravesites, swinging the bones of herself into spaces that did not belong to her, invisible moist bells opened and unfurled in her wake, making the mourners suddenly catch their breaths. She was still-new, which meant that she was not-old. With oiled fairytale tresses. Breasts that were covered but would not be contained. High eyebrows that arched over tight lids as she worked, as she watched the widows shift their eyes beneath hoods of flesh, Mem's mother thinking, almost gloating, *Not me! Not me!*

As Mem got older and grew, the *Not me!* had grown, too. Now, *Not me!* possessed a different, more frantic tone. Papery fans had already begun folding into moon-shapes around a mouth sandwiched between two full parentheses of cheeks, saying, incredulously, *this is the youngest I will ever be*, as if it were a spell that could save her. As if words could stop her flesh from falling from the bone like a chicken cooked long in soup.

Every morning, as Mem's mother applies her daily doses of creams and salves, she peers into the medicine cabinet mirror and gently touches the skin of her face as if it is the face of someone she does not know. She is sure that soon the widows will begin to conspiratorially confide in her or invite her over to tea because they will see, tracking the lines of her face as if it is a map, that she has something in common with them. And once this new kind of attention begins to drift into her life, soft and smug as a consoling pat on the back, the men at gas stations and supermarkets and sidewalks will just as easily stop noticing, stop smiling, stop lending a hand. Withdrawing to notice some brighter, tighter produce.

This is how Mem's mother imagines it will happen: one day she will catch a glimpse of her hurried reflection in a store window, a thumbed-over collage of body parts and smells moving toward an uncontrolled loosening. She'll see her own face withering in its baggy skin, a colorless fruit on the verge of rot, her legendary hair mummified into a beached bed of seaweed pods rattling in the wind. She'll quickly look away. She'll tell herself, *Not me!* and wonder why her hands feel so dry.

While she works, Mem's mother watches the widows with a surgeon's eye. She twists at her handkerchief with not-yet-old hands. She wonders, often, which unseen part of her own self will be the first to wither, then fail. This is why, every night, Mem's mother pats cream onto the swollen crescents under her green eyes and onto the bridge of her Roman nose and peers at herself in the bathroom mirror as if she has already become some-one she does not know, as if the person she does know has been lost or left behind.

But when she opens the medicine cabinet mirror half-way so that it slants against the mirror on the wall and then slides her head between the two mirrors and looks, she sees an endless tunnel of reflections curving out toward an unknown space. A million reflections of reflections of reflec-tions of the person Mem's mother is about to leave behind. Years later, when her daughter asks her to explain the word *infinity*, this is what she will show her.

The bathroom door opens, releasing a flurry of steam and a honeysuckle smell. Through the wet fog Mem can see her mother wrapped in two towels, one on her head, one around her torso. She is slick and soft and gleams like a goddess. She wipes the steam away from the mirrors with the flat of her hand as Mem scrambles to sit on top of the toilet lid with its blue carpet cover. Mem's favorite thing to do is to watch her mother stare at herself in a special face-painting mirror that is round and framed with glowing white bulbs the size of ping-pong balls. The mirror is so powerful you can see the pale down on Mem's mother's cheeks as she concentrates on her reflection, staring at it as if she is searching for something. The mirror has a built-in drawer filled with wondrous and exotic treasures. She fingerpaints her face with colorful goo kept in vials and tubes, or buttery puddles of pudding in pots, using paintbrushes, combs, crayons, and sponges. She pats the top of a bottle onto a fresh white wedge and paints new skin on top of her old skin, covering the faint splatter-shaped birthmark on her forehead. She pulls her brow hairs out with one tool and then draws them back in with another, traces pretend lips on top of her real lips and fills them in with deep red.

Mem thinks that her mother is already the prettiest woman in the world but the pastes and flower-colors make her even more beautiful. *There*, says the satisfied look on the new face of Mem's mother. *That's who I've been looking for all along.*

Mem longs to use her mother's magic paints and glosses, so that she, too, can start as herself, look into the mirror, and end up as someone-else. Sometimes her mother will tap a dot of lipstick onto each of Mem's cheeks and rub it in, but Mem understands that the rest is forbidden, something she will one day be skilled enough to handle. These are things brought in from the outside world of the unprofessionals. They are mysterious, magic, something the regular little girls in her suburban development probably already know how to use. Someday she will master them, too.

Downstairs, on her way into the kitchen, Mem sees a large, square stuffed animal by the front door, leaning against the imitation wrought-iron banister, on top of the scrubbed but still stained linoleum floor. But as Mem comes closer to the animal, she sees the black plastic handles attached and knows it is not an animal at all. It is her mother's packed suitcase, patterned in hairy green-and-red flannel.

If you can't do it, I will have to leave you behind.

"Come in the kitchen, baby," her mother calls. Mem walks into the kitchen, and there is her mother's smile, there is the smoky smell of her hair, there are all of her flushed open pores, and Mem's insides flush in response, urgent, abundant, and too big for her small body to restrain. From that day on, Mem's mother's suitcase remains by the door. It is moved aside each week to clean underneath, but then it goes back in its place. Though Mem's mother takes care to dust it, the bag does fade a bit over the years. The fur by the bottom turns brown and the black handles lose their shine. For twelve years the bag is still and silent but is the loudest thing in the house.

Mem does not want to know what might be inside. When she learns the word *hoary* she pictures the suitcase, though she never touches it. It is not a large bag but to Mem it is monstrous, it stays both on the floor and in Mem's mind, next to the vision of an empty chair, an empty bed, doors permanently closed, all of the things she and her kind are taught to fear. Not the death of their mothers, but the disappearance.

"You are too beautiful for words," her mother says, smiling as she stirs the oatmeal, though she has explained to Mem several times that while being pretty will always help her make money, crying prettily will not. *Professional crying should be like natural crying, ugly and hard to look at, a play of facial contortions that the crier cannot see, including the awkward posture and pose. Clients should find it unbearable to watch yet impossible to turn away, while the Wailer should find it equally as unbearable to be watched. This is the moment you must strive for. It will make you cry harder.*

Around Mem's mother's neck is the locket full of salt from Mem's first baby tears. It's Mem's grandmother's mezuzah, dented from where a neighborhood dog bit it decades ago. Mem's mother knows it's bad luck to wear your children's tears, it's something she would never allow a client to do. But Mem's mother does it anyway. "I love you so much," she says to Mem. "And after today, the rest of the world will love you, too."

She sends Mem out to the front yard to rinse apples, to keep her out of the kitchen. In the morning light the apples are beautiful, a perfect hard redness, and the lawn is dotted with the careless bursts of dandelions mutating into wishes. When Mem finds the hose behind the shrubs and turns it on, the water is hot from lying in its tubing for so long. It spurts out a thick arc that catches the low sun, splashing watery beads across the apples' waxed peels.

Mem lets her eyes unfocus and rest on the soft lawn-wishes and is just deciding which one she will pick to blow when she looks up and sees, gliding down the street, a group of girls from a different court in her development.

But these are not just girls. These are beautiful girls, luscious girls, blond cakes iced from head to toe in glimmery frostings. Mem looks at them and thinks: *puff pastry, lily, foam, milk, moondust, silver, snow.* The tall girl is the shimmeriest, lips painted the color of the inside of an oyster shell, eyelids swirled in mother-of-pearl. Her cheeks are shiny soap bubbles. Even her spun-sugar hair is snowfeathered, puffed into swans wings and silvered at the tips. Her false lips wink and gleam like the rainbow in an oil slick.

The girls are wearing dancer costumes, pink leg-warmers and white jazz shoes, T-shirts artfully torn at the top to reveal glossy shoulders, golden skin spangled with sunlight. Pink and purple ribbons braided into barrettes with small purple beads dangle between stiff meringue peaks of hair. For months Mem has watched these girls sit on the sod-and-curb islands that bulge from the end of each court, carefully plaiting the sherbet-colored ribbons and beads onto plain silver barrettes. Some of them wear roller skates with wide pink laces. The smallest one carries a radio that is almost as big as she is. The iron-on kitten on her T-shirt has chipped and cracked from being washed too much, but it, too, twinkles in the sunlight. As they pass the last island before Mem's house, the tall girl spits a neon-pink wad of gum onto the street.

Even though Mem has never been to school, she knows about these kinds of girls. They always travel in groups of three or four, gliding seamlessly by her house like a parade of confections on a floating platter. At night they catch lightning bugs and dig the lightning part out with their nails while the bugs are still alive, smudging the still-glowing paste into rings around their fingers. Once they spent most of the afternoon singing a song they had made up, to the tune of *The Bridge Over the River Quai*, at the top of their lungs:

> *Herman, look what you've done to me!*
> *Herman, I think it's pregnancy.*
> *Herman, you put your sperm in*
> *And now it's Herman, and Sherman, and me.*

(Later Mem will remember this song with guilty satisfaction. Two of the girls in this group will become pregnant while they are still in high school. As a young teen Mem will watch them, both several pounds heavier, separately walking their babies around the neighborhood in strollers. Neither of the girls will glow anymore. They won't talk to each other. They certainly won't sing.)

Watching this strange bouquet of girls come closer, Mem envisions herself walking down the street with them, laughing their secret laugh, wrapped in pink tatters and floating over the blacktop with roller-skate feet. But when they notice Mem watching, the group stops twittering and hollering to each other, and Mem drops her stare, looking instead at her feet until the girls stop right in front of her. They are so close that when she looks back up she can see the milky grain of their skin and smell their smells: bubblegum, hairspray, nearly grown-up perspiration.

The tall one smiles at Mem, showing all her teeth. Her cheeks are sunrise pink and smooth as a goblet. Her eyes don't flinch when the sun flashes in them.

"Hello!" she says brightly. "What's your name?"

Mem doesn't answer. She has never been asked this before and does not know what to say.

"Don't be scared," the tall girl purrs. "We just want to know your name."

"We've seen you around here," says another. "You don't go to school, right?"

Mem shakes her head *no*.

The tall girl juts out a hip, twirls a piece of golden hair between her fingers. "That's cool. I wish I didn't have to go to school. School sucks. It's like, I don't need to know this stuff. It's *so* stupid. It's *so* gross. You are *so* lucky."

Mem tries to smile. *Cool, sucks, gross.* She doesn't know what any of these words mean. They sound like a secret code.

"You look just like this doll I have," says the big one. "She's supposed to like cry after you give her a bottle and squeeze her belly but she doesn't really like work anymore but that's cool we don't really play with dolls anymore do you have any dolls?"

Mem shakes her head again. She isn't allowed to play with dolls. And she isn't allowed to tell these girls that she isn't allowed to play with dolls. A hot flush opens across her forehead and burns its way down. Maybe this is a test. Maybe her mother is watching from the window, monitoring, making sure that Mem doesn't say the wrong things. But she wants to talk. She wants to tell them how pretty she thinks they are, that they look like dolls, too. She pokes her toes into the grass.

"So, do you want to be our friend?" asks the tall girl, and Mem nods *yes*.

"What's your name?" asks the girl.

Mem has no idea what to say. Before she can answer, the small girl starts to laugh. She smiles gently at Mem, asking in a kind voice, "Are you a *retard*?"

"My name is Mirabelle," Mem answers quickly, and even as she says it she knows it sounds like a lie. Behind her the spigot hisses.

"Oh," says the tall one. "*Mirabelle.*"

She cocks her pretty head to the side and smiles so hard her gums show.

"Well, Mirabelle," she says, "you smell. Do you know that?"

"She does, she smells," says the tall girl to the rest, who nod seriously in agreement. "It's her ugly, pukey, gypsy feet that smell. I guess she does-n't know how to shower."

As the girls walk around Mem like creatures picking over carrion, Mem looks down at her feet, the dancing-feet-of-joy that had sent her spinning around the kitchen the night before. And then she sees that what they say is true. Her toes are small and dirty and shaped like grubs. They are horrible feet! Terrible feet, the skin white as salt cod. Mem can see the map of veins under the pallid flesh. She tries to cover one foot with the other, burying her toes into the dirt.

The big one calls Mem *Crybaby*.

"Make her cry," says the one carrying the radio. "Go ahead. I bet she loves to cry."

Mem wishes her mother were here. Her mother would know what to do. She would say something funny and smart, something that would get their respect. Something that would make them want to be her friend.

But Mem's mother is not there.

"Here," Mem says as she bends over. She hands the big girl a clean, new apple, still damp and ruby red.

They take the apples and smile, kindly. Real smiles.

They ask Mem to join their group.

"Mirabelle," they say, "what a beautiful name."

But they only bare their teeth, like any animal saying to its prey, *You are food*.

The tall one wrinkles her small nose at the apple in her hand and pre-tends to sniff it.

"Did she touch this?" she asks her friends, not looking at Mem. "Did that smelly freak touch this? Yeah, I bet she touched these apples. Because they smell like shit."

She drops her apple as if it is hot and has burned her and the others follow suit, pulling apples up from the lawn and then dropping them, plop plop plop. The little one throws hers at the side of Mem's house. Then they start to whisper their secret whispers and giggle their secret giggles and they draw themselves together and float away like cream.

Mem chews on her lip and tries to wash the pulp off the ground without looking at her awful feet or inhaling her shitty smell. She feels like the scummy *schmutz* on the top of soup. She feels like the part of the deceased they vacuum out and throw away.

But she is also going to be a star. She will make millions of dollars before any of these girls even figure out what they want to do with their silly lives. She will be a legend someday. She will be a Master. She will attend the funerals of each of these girls and make a fortune off of their demise. Maybe she will spit on their graves.

When Mem goes back into her room to change, she finds her first set of blacks hanging by the molding around her bedroom doorway and forgets about the girls and the things they have said. She is finally getting her first real doole—black taffeta with a full, starched skirt—embroidered with tiny blue flowers around the collar and cuffs. Forget-me-nots, the mourner's flower, the traditional emblem of her kind. There are also matching black Mary Janes, hard and glossy as ladybug's wings, and a pair of white tights rolled up into a ball. They feel just like their name when she puts them on, a dry skin that doesn't fit. They wrinkle at the ankles and knees.

Before breakfast, Mem's mother brushes Mem's fine dark hair and smiles. "On the morning of my First Funeral my mother wouldn't even let me have breakfast," she says. "She thought not eating might make me cranky so I would weep harder. Really, it just made me more nervous. Ayin wasn't old enough to go to the job so she was allowed to eat. She had french toast and milk and chewed with her mouth open so that I could watch every bite."

"That was mean," says Mem.

Mem's mother stops smiling. She puts the brush down and looks at her daughter.

"You wouldn't have lasted two weeks with my mother," she says.

Mem's mother's freshly painted false mouth suddenly makes the face look like someone else, a mask she has made and can't take off. The some-one-else says, "Go eat your breakfast," as if the softness of Mem's mother has hardened, dark along the edges like a cheese left out too long.

Hanging on the hallway wall across from Mem's room is a framed photograph of Mem's grandmother. In the picture she looks very small and tired, unlike the raging giantess Aunt Ayin and her mother are always describing. She seems surprised to be having her photograph taken, even though it is a studio shot with a smoky background, her astonished face a waterfall of shirred skin with two almond-shaped eyes peeking through. She has a puff of wig-like hair dyed shoe-polish black. The edges of the photograph are watercolor brown, as if they have been dipped in very weak tea.

Mem doesn't like this picture. She never knew her grandmother, a nationally renowned apprentice-trainer who died in a mysterious fire when Mem's mother was only seventeen years old. Sometimes, when it is dark after suppertime and Mem is walking alone through the hallway, she thinks the woman in the picture is watching, beady eyes shifting as Mem walks by.

You wouldn't have lasted two weeks with my mother.

Mem doesn't doubt for a second that this is true.

Mem's new shoes tap the linoleum floor in the kitchen with a delicious water-dripping, finger-snapping sound. The oatmeal in Mem's bowl is full of raisins that have bloated from the hot milk into fat ticks. Mem pokes at them with her spoon. She remembers the story of Aunt Ayin's First Funeral, how Ayin giggled from nerves as soon as the mourners arrived, the giggling getting louder and harder to control, even when she smothered her mouth with her handkerchief. When they had all come home from the funeral that day, Mem's grandmother had dragged Aunt Ayin into the bathroom by the neck of her doole, pushed her head into the toilet, and flushed three times.

Mem swirls a lump of bright yellow margarine into her oatmeal as her mother comes in to join her. Mem's mother is wearing her best blacks, her most expensive doole, a raw silk shift with carved black buttons all the way down the front. It is one of several dozen dooles Mem's mother keeps hung neat and straight in her closet, with the hooks of the hangers all going in the same direction. She usually decides in advance which she will wear depending on who has died, what religion they were, and how much money the survivors are willing to pay. Today, like most days, is a high-fee doole day.

"I'm talking to you, baby," says Mem's mother.

Mem is listening while she picks the ticks out of her oatmeal with her fingers and puts them on a napkin. Their little feet wriggle.

"You know how much I love you," says Mem's mother. "You know how proud I am of you. You are beautiful and strong." But when Mem looks up she sees the someone-else's meticulously painted mouth open and shriek, "*You lazy fucking pig!*"

A bruise-colored monster mouth.

"*Little lazy whore! I wish I never had you!*"

Bigger than Mem's whole face.

"*I'm so ashamed of you I could vomit!*"

Opening and closing, spitting, retching.

"*You've been nothing but a goddamned waste!*"

The ugliest thing Mem has ever seen.

Her mother's small teeth and pink tongue work the air like a machine, rouged jowls squeezing the mouth, fleshy lips flapping, shape-making. Coming at her, getting bigger and bigger until she is a blur, pressing her own forehead against Mem's forehead. Pushing. "*Look at yourself! No wonder your father left! You're a fucking disgrace!*"

Mem feels the oatmeal lumping up on the roof of her mouth. The skin tightening around her face. The sudden stickiness of all her creases. There is the smoky smell of her mother's hair and there are all of her pores. Mem can't tell where her skin ends and her mother's begins because Mem's mother is the size of the house. Bigger than the house. There is no end to her.

But then it stops. Mem's mother pulls back, smiling. She smoothes a curl of hair with her fingers and takes a sip of coffee from a mug decorated with small, grinning cats. She looks at Mem, carefully. Her fingernails are the color of blood.

She asks, "How do you feel, honey?"

Mem can't answer. She doesn't know how she is supposed to feel. Has she not loved her mother enough? Has she been eating the oatmeal the wrong way? Is it something she said, or did, or didn't say or do?

Her mother's face looks suddenly sad and scared. In a little girl's voice she says, "I don't really believe that you love me. Do you? Do you love me?"

Mem nods earnestly, urgently, how can her mother not know this?

"Good!" says Mem's mother brightly, smiling her normal pleased smile. "Now my beautiful girl is ready to prove she is a star. Now we can go to work."

Mem's mother puts the dishes in the sink. Hustle and bustle. Receipts, names, directions. Handkerchiefs. Lipstick, keys. Like everything is okay.

As they walk toward the door, Mem's mother makes a sharp noise of delight and points at the ceiling. Dangling by the molding, just beneath a fracture in the wood, is a small brown spider, arduously weaving a single line downward.

Plumb straight.

Sparkling spun.

An old sign of money to come.

— 1983 A.D., PENNSYLVANIA, UNITED STATES —

Excerpt of a Statement
by State Representative Anthony J. DePaul, Jr. (R-13th)

Support for a Prohibition of Professional Mourning in the Commonwealth of Pennsylvania

"As leaders of state, we are obliged to remember that it is our virtue which separates us from other earthly creatures, a unique and God-given ability to create value systems and to then make choices based upon those systems; in honor of this virtue, I now appeal to the integrity of my colleagues and constituents to help eradicate the immoral practice of 'professional mourning' from our Commonwealth...

We can no longer allow the behaviors of those who knowingly refuse to abide by the laws of this state and the principles of human decency to carry on; the adults concerned are child-abusers and scofflaws who neglect and exploit their own innocent children for profit, then rear the youth to perpetuate the cycle. I have witnessed this intolerable corruption with my own eyes and am still haunted by the image of two very young and frightened girls pinching their own arms and biting their lips to make themselves cry. They were obviously and understandably terrified...

Unfortunately, my experience was not an isolated incident. Similar reports have been made concerning burials in Norfolk, Boston, Jacksonville, Florida, and throughout southern New Jersey. This is inexcusable; every decent citizen and representative should be outraged; we must demand change; we must uphold the very principles our elected stations were designed to protect..."

4

"Is it true they make you fondle corpses?"

Going from the air-conditioned house to the warmth outside feels good at first. The summer heat drapes itself over Mem's cool arms as she scrambles into the backseat of her mother's big silver car. But once in the car, Mem feels a thick and sinuous worry creep its way through her veins like embalming fluid. Mem worries about her tights falling down, about not being able to cry, about the things she might have done to make her mother so angry.

This is the graveyard, she remembers her mother saying, *colors come and go but the one that stays is gray. The unprofessionals are already half-corpses, the putrefaction began years ago when the bones stopped growing. They can smell it on themselves in the early mornings and late at night, they try to scrub it away or cover it up. Their bathrooms are full of products made to preserve skin, hair, teeth, nails, gums, bones, like bottles and pastes of embalming fluid, and someone is making a fortune off of their slow dying.*

Inside it is hot enough to smell the cracked seat cushions oozing their tufts of yellow stuffing. She picks at the stuffing and wonders what she will do if someone at the funeral asks for her name.

Mem. Mirabelle. Mem. Mirabelle.

Filth. Whore. Lazy. Liar.

Mem.

Aunt Ayin said that Mem was born under the perfect sign for a Master

Wailer—Aquarius—a water bearer with small feet. Alchemical symbol for multiplication and salt niter. With a 3-line trigram drawn by Aunt Ayin on the day of Mem's birth and taped to the pink hearts and daisies of the newly wallpapered wall:

—— —

——————

——————

Meaning: *Sorceress, Joy, Reflections, Salt.*

As they pull from the driveway, Mem pokes at the flaked-off vinyl and hard piping ruptured like a half-done operation. Under her feet, one of the bald tires thumps a steady rhythm in its well.

No Wonder

No Wonder

No Wonder Your Father Left

Mem's mother's anger is there in the car with them, damp, with coarse edges and pith, like drying cement. To distract herself from it, Mem twists around to watch the development shrink past. From the back window Mem's neighborhood is a chain of paper dolls shaped like houses. The top halves of the houses are covered with siding in *Robin's Egg, Summer Sand,* or *Lemon Mist,* and the bottom halves are made of dark maroon bricks, marrow-colored, the same shade women were wearing on their lips and nails when the houses were built. Mem's mother's house is yellow. When the wind blows against the siding at night, the metal strips vibrate, groaning like an old ship at sea.

Mem's mother was able to buy the house in cash, just before Mem was born, using a lifetime of Master-level fees. When she first moved in, the dead-end court was buffeted at both ends by wraparound woods with a gurgling creek threaded through it. Daisies and Queen Anne's lace and tall, languorous grasses grew at each mouth of the woods. Acres of corn fields surrounded the woods that surrounded the development. At night you could hear anxious courting grasshoppers, the flurry of birds, small four-legged things rustling the grass as they stalked.

That first year, as the months passed, the sounds around the house changed. The woods began to steadily disappear, as if a virus had blighted them out. Bulldozers ground their gears during the day and sat smug in their mounds of earth by night, slaughtered daisies and Queen Anne's lace and tall onion grasses strewn across their fronts like exhausted protesters. New hand-in-hand houses went up, just as quickly as the woods had come down. Now at night Mem's mother hears neighbors' dishes clinking as they are washed, children hollering as they play, people arguing. Cars starting. Cars pulling up. Car doors opening and closing. And the vacant, half-expectant suburban sound of nothing at all.

They pull out of the development and drive down Mem's favorite street, a single-lane road snake-shaped with rollercoaster humps. As the car drives up and then down the humps, Mem's belly thrills with an electric caved-in feeling and the coils of her mother's long hair bounce like springs. Mem taps her fingernails against the pistachio shells stuffed in the little backseat ashtrays from the previous owners. Once on the highway the car passes a cloud factory lit up with a thousand white lights, curds of noxious steam billowing from several stacks. "P.U.!" cries Mem's mother, rolling up her window as fast as she can, but it is too late, the smell is already inside the car. "P.U.!" says Mem. They both laugh.

Then Mem's mother stops laughing. Her voice gets hard.

"That's the reason so many women here have breast cancer," she says.

The sweaty backs of Mem's knees mix with the plastic and turn gluey, making sucking noises when she moves. The hard cracks in the plastic pinch her skin. She sits up straight once they start down the Roosevelt Boulevard so she can watch all of the sad, static people waiting for buses, the skinny boys on the medians in between the lanes hawking newspapers, roses, stuffed animals, soft pretzels covered in small pellets of bright white salt. The boys are all tan and tired. The soft pretzels look wilted, but good, and Mem can almost taste their chewy saltiness, the tang of grainy brown mustard on top.

On one corner hazard lights flash. A SEPTA bus has broken down, full of hot and irritated people who will have to wait until another bus comes to save them.

"Mommy look at all those people stuck on the bus," says Mem.

Mem's mother doesn't look. She sighs, wiping her forehead with her wrist.

"At least we're not those people," she says.

As the car pulls into the parking lot next to Hector Paul's funeral home, Mem's mother sighs again. She says, as if to herself, "Thank god we can always count on Hector. Thank god he's such a tit-man. At least I still have something."

Mem opens her door and climbs out of the car. The tar running along the edge of the road is soft and malleable, like a huge black wad of already-chewed gum. Aunt Ayin and Sofie are waiting at the entrance of the funeral parlor, standing under an awning framed by two white pillars. In her new blacks, Sofie looks like a long-ago photograph of someone's grandmother as a little girl, pale cheeks a just-kneaded dough. She is pallid and fidgety in an unyielding bell-shaped doole, looking smaller than usual as she stands next to her mother.

Aunt Ayin gave birth to Sofie exactly two days and three months before Mem was born, an event which transformed her overnight into an authority on motherhood and domesticity, though Ayin never cleans her flaking, almost-unfurnished one-bedroom apartment and keeps anything of value packed in stained cardboard boxes by the front door *in case of fire or other emergencies*. Unlike Mem, Sofie came into the world weeping, twitching with the effort of having been born, small and jaundiced. She came out crying and rarely stopped, calling out her lukewarm protests with her thin legs kicking, muttering weak cries even at the breast, even in her sleep. She wouldn't go down for more than a few moments at a time and would wake and start at the slightest creak of the floorboards.

"Crying is food for you, it's like medicine," Aunt Ayin had said. "If you keep it bottled up you can get sick."

Secretly Mem's mother hoped that her own child wouldn't be so sensitive, so nervous and lactose intolerant. She remembered how easily Aunt

Ayin had cried as a child. But Aunt Ayin didn't mind Sofie's crying. It meant, she said, that her daughter would become a star. She picked up the baby as often as she could, holding her close against her straining buttons and cooing at her daughter's contorted face. She was careful not to squeeze too much, though; she remembered how as a toddler she had once hugged a kitten so hard she smothered it to death.

"You'd better teach her how to stop," Mem's mother warned when Sofie was just a few days old. "You know the trouble that comes from not being able to stop."

"Oh, *shah*, she's just testing out her pipes," Aunt Ayin had said, jovially bouncing the weepy baby Sofie against her mammoth breasts.

In front of Hector Paul's funeral home, Aunt Ayin smiles bovinely, her wide face crimson and shiny as egg-washed plaits of challah, and Mem has to control the desperate urge that possesses her every time she looks up at her aunt, a relentless yearning to stick her fingers into Ayin's invitingly large, round nostrils. Aunt Ayin shifts her weight, her bulges straining against the buttons of her doole. She huffs and heaves and yanks at the taut fabric of her dress and touches her damp hair, which is curly brown like Mem's mother's but plain and coarse instead of shiny. When Aunt Ayin was a little girl her mother insisted she wear olive oil in her hair to make it soft. When they went to visit other Wailers' houses Ayin was not allowed to sit on any of the good furniture. Now Aunt Ayin refuses to even cook with olive oil, she says the smell makes her sick, and when she has her hair cut she keeps the leftover locks in a box so that no one can cast a hex on her.

It's easy to understand where Ayin's superstitions come from: when she was just a plump girl of sixteen, she cried in the dark corners of her room and prayed for something terrible to happen and it did.

Her sister was beautiful, with thick dark hair that never needed oil. She performed brilliantly, heart-breakingly, at the drop of a hat. One day, when Aunt Ayin was pretending to cry and had started to wail, Ayin's mother leaned over and spat right into Ayin's open mouth. That night, after her sister had fallen asleep with slices of cold cucumber on her eyes to help keep the swelling down, Ayin weaved her fingers together over her generous belly and, weeping for real, begged Aurora for something to happen to make her sister go away. Her tears dripped down her face and got caught in the fold between her two chins, and as she moved her hand to wipe them away, she smelled smoke.

Their mother died in the fire, suffocating in her sleep. As the two girls stood on the sidewalk, stunned into disbelief as the smell and the sirens and the heat engulfed them, Ayin knew that it had been her wish for catastrophe that had made it happen. She knew then that there were forces in the world much stronger than herself, and that she would always have to respect them. In this way, standing on the curb with her large bare feet growing colder and colder, Ayin submitted to the mysterious powers of the universe, vowing to honor and fear them for the rest of her life.

"Today," Aunt Ayin says, "the morning is full of good signs—and what wonderful weather for the girls' First Funeral!" Although, she notes, it's better to work on colder days. "It's more authentic." She pictures long black cloaks billowing, portentous gray clouds, wet handkerchiefs trembling between bitter blue fingertips, raw, red noses. The other Wailers say that Aunt Ayin has an active imagination, but Mem's mother thinks that her sister is just scatterbrained. In Yiddish she calls her *ugalust*.

The parlor door opens. A thin man with a well-sprayed comb-over and a mustache skinny as a lady's eyebrow invites them all to step inside, greeting Mem's mother and Aunt Ayin with subdued enthusiasm. His voice is soft and soothing, a hum, more musical instrument than voice. He says hello to Mem and hello to Sofie and leads them down a long hallway toward the viewing room.

"I can't thank you enough for this, Hector," says Mem's mother, smoothing her curls with her fingers.

Hector tilts his head and smiles gently. "Think nothing of it," he says. "I understand how important it is to get the girls accustomed." He glances down at Mem, smiling benevolently. "Perhaps we can look forward to the debut of another Master today, no?"

Mem tries to look at him and return the smile, but Hector's pale green eyes seem to be focused in two different directions, as if one might be broken, and Mem isn't sure which eye to look at so instead she looks down, watches her new shoes march across the soft teal runners. The runners muffle her footsteps so that she can't even hear herself walking. Brushed brass sconces cast timid yellow halos on the floors and walls. Mem has never been in such a silent place, it is as if the air is made of pillows. She is afraid that if she says anything at all, even if she whispers, it will sound like yelling. She uses every drop of her energy to keep her mouth closed.

Hector opens a large white door with brass handles and leads them into a small room. There are a few teal sofa-chairs and a polished wooden casket that has brass handles, too. Seeing this, Sofie's face grows like a picture on a balloon that is being blown up.

A glass bowl on one of the low tables is filled with candies in wrappers that say *Testamints*, with the capital "T" shaped like a cross. Mem's mother pushes one of the sofa-chairs up against the side of the coffin and motions for Mem to come closer. "This is a corpse, Mem," she says. "This is the deceased. You remember we talked about the deceased? I need you to look at him, get a good look, before they go to bury him."

Mem looks at her mother. Soft mouth. Soft face. Love radiates from her. Everything is okay now.

Her mother swoops down, picking Mem up by the waist, and stands her on the sofa-chair. Looking down, Mem sees an old, not-breathing man in a dark suit lying in a crib of baby blue satin. He is wearing more make-up than her mother.

"I see you're using the new extremities arranger," Mem's mother says to Hector, looking very impressed. To Mem she says, "His name was Frank. He was seventy years old. He had a heart attack."

Heart attack. Did he love someone too much until his heart exploded? Did no one love him, so his heart stopped? Mem puts her hand over her own heart, she feels it thump against her ribs like a small animal that wants to get out. *Heart attack.* It seems to Mem like a perfectly plausible way to die.

"Did the heart attack hurt?" asks Mem.

Her mother nods absently. She says, "It always hurts to die."

Mem looks again at the thick skin dotted with dense whiskers trying to come up from underneath, the bulbous nose and wide, flat eyebrows coarse as toothbrush bristles. She hasn't seen too many men this close up. She has heard some Aunts say that all men are monsters. Mem's mother believes instead that all grown men are little boys who do not know what they want or how to give a woman what she needs. *Although you may lay down with men so as to take their seed and provide yourself with daughters*, she has explained, *that is all that men are good for and therefore all you should ever do with them. Men are always lost, they are confused and afraid, thus they are more trouble than they're worth.*

Also, they are stupid and cannot truly feel. They can pay for tears but cannot manufacture them. Because they have learned as small boys how to feel nothing but humor and anger, the only way men of any age can get away with crying in public is to look like they are trying not to. Their public tears make them claustrophobic, but in private, men try to seek out small places to enjoy their grief: closets, bathrooms, corners, bingeing and purging their sobs where no one else will see. Because of this, men can never be professionals and therefore tend to not take Wailers as seriously as they should.

Frank's eyes will never cry again, although they will soon liquefy and drip out. His lips have been sewn together with thin black stitches, and Mem knows that his face has been roughly massaged and re-shaped to look serene because rigor mortis causes muscle contractions that distort all of the features. Mem wishes she could have seen that face instead of this one.

"They took out his insides, his *kishkas*, and filled him up with chemicals so he won't decompose," Mem's mother explains. It's easy to see that she's pleased Mem isn't squeamish. "His cheeks are filled with stuffing, like a pillow, to make his face look more natural."

"Did *that* hurt, too?" asks Mem.

"No, no, sweetheart, you don't feel anything after you're dead, remember? It's just a body, with nothing inside of it anymore. The person he was isn't inside of him anymore. Now it's nothing. A shell. Go ahead and touch," Mem's mother instructs, briefly running her own fingers over the dead man's cheek. "So you can see he's not a living thing anymore, just a shell. I want you to feel it so that you won't be scared."

Mem bends over and gently places her hand against the dead man's made-up forehead. She is surprised by how cool the skin feels. It doesn't feel like a shell. It feels like an uncooked chicken—hard, with spongy skin.

"Soon it will be all bones," says Mem's mother. "And then dust."

Mem takes her hand away and her mother smiles, kisses her twice. She whispers, "You're so beautiful. You're already a professional, not afraid at all."

Mem and Sofie had learned just that week about the horrible fears of the unprofessionals. Fear of a Painful and Lonely Death, Fear of a Humiliating Death, Fear of Posthumous Exposure & Embarrassment, Fear of Premature Burial, Fear of Bodily Putrefaction, Fear of Being Forgotten. The unprofessionals were so riddled with these fears that they became obsessed, but they were so afraid to even think about dying that they never managed to plan things out or practice *ars moriendi*, the art of dying well.

"What happens after you die?" Mem had asked her mother after the Lesson was finished. Mem's mother had been standing with her back to Mem, chopping onions for the kugel on the counter. "No one knows," she said. "What's important is what happens while you're alive. Don't waste time thinking about those things. It's not important."

But to Mem it is very important. Extremely important. Especially because Mem understands that if there aren't any horrible car accidents or wars, her mother is probably going to die before she does. Mem without her mother would be a lost and floating balloon. A puppet without a puppeteer.

Sometimes Mem thinks she should ask Aunt Ayin about what happens after you die, since Ayin is so keen to tell stories and ancestors' tales. But Mem is sure that Ayin would not really know the answer herself, and would instead invent some flowery fiction. It also might be true that Aunt Ayin simply doesn't like Mem, and wouldn't tell her anyway. Taken out of context, Aunt Ayin's stories, always spring-loaded with old-world lessons, seem to be the kind of stories an aunt should tell a niece she loves.

Charming fables. Mystical myths. Sweet parables lovingly told, saved up and doled out on special occasions, like silver dollars.

But Mem knows better. When Aunt Ayin tells Mem Wailers' tales there is an urgency, a sweaty self-absorption that has nothing to do with Mem or her quiet attention. Aunt Ayin speaks as if rehearsing lines for a play, her animated hands and face at an angle titling just a little bit away from Mem, her eyes fixed on something else, a table leg, a calendar on the wall, shrubs in front of the window. Although Mem is the only niece she knows it does not mean that she is the favorite niece, or even a niece who is loved. Still, Mem listens to Aunt Ayin during the Lessons and watches her flabby silhouette as she speaks, and sometimes Mem smiles, believing the stories, and is full of questions she knows she will never be able to ask.

"Okay, Sofie," Mem's mother says firmly, helping Mem off the sofa-chair in front of Frank's casket. "Now it's your turn."

Mem tries to send a message to Sofie without using her mouth. *It's okay*, she says to Sofie with her eyes. *Don't be scared.* But Sofie isn't listening. She is sucking her thumb and staring at her mother and twirling a piece of dark hair around her finger. Her face is whiter than the walls in the room.

"You know she's going to ruin her teeth doing that," says Mem's mother to Aunt Ayin.

"Go on," murmurs Aunt Ayin, giving Sofie a little shove. But Sofie won't move. Mem hears a sizzling, a low hiss coming from Sofie's ankles as Aunt Ayin cries, "Oh no, Sofie!"

But there is already a dark teal puddle on the carpet around Sofie's wet Mary Janes. Hector is already running on tiptoe to fetch some paper towels. Sofie is already crying, her open mouth gasping, wailing. Poor Sofie. This is not the first time, Mem knows. Every day she hears Sofie's plastic underwear crackling under her dress. She smells the accidents, strong and yellow and chemical. But she never says anything. "Oh, for Christ's sake," snorts Mem's mother. "Ayin, get control of your daughter, would you?" She stands there, not helping, and shakes her head. Mem is relived that her mother's disgust is not for her. She feels bad for Sofie but secretly she is grateful that this has happened, that the order of things has been restored. Mem is again the good one, her dryness a virtue instead of a curse.

Hector calmly strolls back into the room, armed with two rolls of paper towels and a can of carpet cleaner. "It's no problem, really," he hums, handing a roll of paper towels to Aunt Ayin. "You can use the private bathroom to clean her up." He cautiously bends onto one knee and begins tearing off several sheets of paper towels as Aunt Ayin hurries Sofie out of the room.

Sighing mildly, Hector chuckles to himself, one eye looking at the wall, the other eye looking up at Mem's mother, who is about to apologize. He puts up his hand. His fingers are girlishly long and slender. "Don't bother, my dear, it's perfectly all right," he says. "After all, you're the best contractor I've ever had. This is all water under the bridge, so to speak." He laughs at his own joke and shakes the can of carpet cleaner over the wet spot.

"So, that little Sofia," he says. "She's a wet one, isn't she?"

— 1885 A.D., TORONTO, CANADA —

attributed to Keith Christopher Bruce

Beware the Grim Weepers

If a loved one soon should pass
(One of virtue and good deeds)
Beware the shy and lovely lass
Who's donned in mourning weeds.

She'll call the night you lose your old
And mock a studied gloom
But 'fore the corpse is even cold
She'll step into the room.

She'll plead, *Hire me for whom you've lost*
By gravesite I shall wail
A tribute—at a modest cost—
An honorable sale.

The light will gleam against her cheek
As rivulets they'll flow
Then, grief unbound, her eyes will leak
To display her sorrow.

But be not fooled, O mourners fair,
For though her tears seem true,
She'll use this craft of wet despair
While she is robbing you.

Her kith and kin have thrived and spread
Across this globe's blue waters,

Taught to shame and rob our dead
While breeding wicked daughters.

She takes advantage of your grief
(Your loss is her good gain)
And, like any common thief,
She leaves you naught but pain.

She'll seize your gold, your coins and wealth
While you're gripped with despair
Then steal your dignity and health
And leave without a care!

Beware this wench of misery!
Take heed her howls and tears!
Do not employ this sly gypsy
When burying your dears.

Instead, hire he who digs the holes
To raise and swing his shovels,
And frighten all these wretched souls
Back to their dank hovels.

5

"How do you make yourself cry on cue?"

M em can still feel the chicken-skin of Frank's dead face on her fingers
as she walks through the cemetery. She studies the tombstones as
she strides up the rolling green hills. Some of the stones are shaped like
angels or spires or open books, though most just stick up out of the ground
like dirty buck teeth. A few are as big as the shed on the side of Mem's
house, big dollhouses made of slick marble veined with white. She wishes
she could touch the walls of one of the marble sheds, let her hand slide
against the cool stone to erase the feeling in her fingertips.

Mem gazes at the beautiful green hills full of boxes of dead people
decomposing. She is a little bothered by all of this burying, planting dead
bodies like root bulbs in their Sunday best. What is going to happen when
they run out of room? Soon there won't be any place on earth where there
isn't someone buried under the dry crust of dirt. Children digging for
China in their backyards will find teeth and navy blue suit jackets. Grazing
deer will nip at the grass and pull up finger bones. The roads will rattle
under cars like maracas. Mem can almost hear the sound: cadavers chatter-
ing under the tires of her mother's car. Underground dancing bones. And
dust. How long will it take for Frank to turn into dust? Is that what all dust
is made of? Mem thinks about the lint in the pockets of her jeans at home,
the way the dust motes dance in the late-day spears of light by her bedroom window. *D* for *Dancing Dust*. *D* for *Decompose*. *D* for *Dead*.

In the distance, Mem hears the circus-music rhythm of a car alarm going off. "How are we supposed to work under these conditions?" says Aunt Ayin, tossing her dimpled hands up in the air. "Tchaikovsky didn't have to be concerned with the wailing of car alarms interfering with his composition."

Mem's mother points to another job in progress, ahead and to the left of the cemetery path, where the mourners are huddled around a canopied hole. Mem's mother cranes her neck to see who is working it but it's too far away to tell. They hear a few melodramatic wails pealing from the site. As they get closer Mem sees two older Wailers doing their best; one has ripped the bodice of her doole. The other one's face is streaked with teary mascara, long black lines striping her face like war paint.

Mem's mother scoffs. "Gypsy tricks," she says. Aunt Ayin agrees. "It's unprofessional," she sniffs.

Mem's mother has already explained to Mem how such women use low-rate (unprofessional, inauthentic) artifice, tearing their dooles in advance and then stitching them back together with weak thread, strategically placing the rents where the cloth will give easily. They wear extra layers of makeup that are not waterproof and rub their fingers with onion or soap so they can make themselves cry and their makeup will run. A low-rate Wailer will even collect clumps of her own hair from combs or brushes and use fake eyelash glue to stick the clumps to her scalp, so she can pretend to pull them out during the funeral.

"It's a disgrace to the profession. Completely inauthentic. What would the ancestors say?" asks Mem's mother, her lips screwed into the shape of *tsk*.

She looks down at Mem when they reach their job site. "Promise me you'll never do any of those cheap tricks, ever. Promise me you'll remember," she says, and Mem nods. "Your tears are ancestral. They are uncommon and come with a certificate of pedigree. They're exceptional. And they will never come cheap."

Mem remembers the story about her great-great-great cousins in France who died in droves before the Revolution, accidentally poisoned through the hands from clutching lead coffins as they wailed. Even then they used last breaths on death beds to whisper the Lessons so that once the Revolution finally arrived and all the lead coffins were dug up for bullets, the good daughters who remembered the whispers were prepared to profit from losses to come.

At the site, there are already two other Wailers standing among the cross-shaped garlands, a woman and a girl Mem has never seen before. Both have long hair colorless as corn silks and a scattering of freckles across the bridges of their noses. They wear full blacks, standing on the real grass next to a mound of earth covered by a blanket of fake grass. The girl delicately picks her nose when her mother looks away.

"Who's that?" asks Sofie. She smells faintly of urine and Aunt Ayin's tea rose perfume.

Mem's mother smiles at the two Wailers, her smile saying, *I will be polite to you but do not forget who I am.* She tells Mem their secret names: *Aunt Binah, Derasha.* Mem stares at Derasha's hair, her elegant ears shaped like teacup handles. Derasha stares back while the mothers talk shop. She is a full head taller than Mem.

Oh, I know who you're talking about, she has amazing stamina, Mem hears her mother say to Aunt Binah. *She had a strange bout of dry-eye there for a while in the seventies but she's rolling in dough now.*

Mem politely asks Derasha if this is her First Funeral.

"No," Derasha replies, tossing her pale hair over one shoulder. "I'm not a baby."

"Oh," says Mem. "How old are you?"

Derasha's blue eyes consider Mem with contempt. She taps her own shiny Mary Janes impatiently against the grass.

Then her cousin put that poor little boy in a doole and brought him to the McCrary funeral in Cherry Hill. As if no one would notice!

"I'm nine. I can whistle and I can blow bubbles with gum," Derasha says finally. "Can you?"

Mem shakes her head. She isn't allowed to chew gum.

Drunk, Mem hears Aunt Binah say. *I can't stand working with her. Her sister actually brings a harmonica to the jobs to make sure they're both wailing at C-sharp pitch. You can smell the Jack Daniels from the other side of the hole.*

Derasha flicks her head to the other side and her hair flows like an underwater creature, tails made of sunlight. "I'm going to be a famous actress," she says.

They did such a shoddy embalming job that those awful phorid flies were everywhere.

"Wow," says Mem, very impressed.

It was six, no, seven before they changed the law last month, says Aunt Ayin. *Now it's only three at a time, not including children, thank god. But who's checking?*

"And my family's from the House of Marcella in Rome where St. Jerome visited all the widows and taught them Hebrew," says Derasha. "We're a legend."

At least we can get health insurance this year, replied Aunt Binah. *My youngest just had chicken pox. Now they're all going to get it.*

Mem is about to tell Derasha that her family is a legend, too, when she sees a polished gray hearse leading a slow caravan of cars into the cemetery. All the cars have neon orange stickers on the windows. They slowly snake around the hill at the bottom, and then stop. Mem's mother moves behind the girls, nodding quickly to Mem as she passes. Doors open, doors shut, there are some murmurs, loud breathing. About a dozen whispering mourners make their way up the hills, all in black, shrugged together like stooped shoulders. Some of the women are wearing short skirts and pointy high heels that sink into the ground as they walk. They try to look serene and sad while they teeter and wobble up the hill. Mem gets nervous all over again and tries to make her face look somber. Mournful. She frowns and sighs and knits her brows.

"Stop making faces," her mother says.

What happens next goes by very quickly, a gathering and a rustling, like fallen leaves settling. "That's the widow," whispers Derasha, nodding toward a woman wearing a stern black suit and black heels with buckles.

The widow's arms sag against other people's arms, her hair straggling away from its bun. The other mourners follow, everyone wearing their serious faces, heads bent, hands clasped awkwardly.

Mem is able to make out the priest as he walks by because of his robe and the book he holds beneath his crossed arms. Although he might be a vicar or a minister, Mem doesn't know the difference yet. *Don't worry about it, they're professionals, like us,* her mother has explained. *They're at the jobs to make money, too. They'll completely ignore you. Just ignore them back.*

The mourners arrange themselves around the hole, barely noticing that Wailers are there. Mem can't see anything but legs and black shoes. Polished patent leather. Old loafers. Careful cuffs and stockings the color of smoke. When the priest begins to talk, he uses Hector's humming voice. Mem can't quite make out what he is saying. She strains to listen but all she hears clearly is the word *God*, over and over again. Her doole begins to soak up heat from the sun, trapping it between the starched layers. Her mother—all three of the mothers—is standing right behind them, in back of everyone else. They don't say a word. Soft dandelion wishes pirouette past Mem, riding a breeze only they can feel. She wants to reach out and catch one, let its furriness collapse between her fingers, make her wish, let it go. She would wish to never inherit her grandmother's curse, the horrible Sjogren's syndrome that squeezes a Wailer's lachrymal glands into hard, dry pits that cannot cry. What if, instead of leaking prosperity, Mem's tear ducts block themselves up and only dribble, disappointingly, like a broken faucet?

"What are we supposed to do?" whispers Sofie, wide-eyed, panicked. Mem listens for some signal from the mothers—a sniffle, a sob, a blown nose—but all she hears are the birds chirping, cars passing, the sound of people's shoes shifting on the grass.

"*Now?*" Mem asks Derasha, who is staring straight ahead.

"No, not now," she says.

Across the street is a billboard that reads: *If You Lived Here, You'd Already Be Home.* Mem knows what is waiting for her at home. Empty bags waiting to be packed full. A big house where her mother won't be living anymore. How will Mem feed herself if she can't even reach the cupboards in the kitchen? How will she do the laundry, pay the bills, run a bath?

She won't have to. Once her mother is gone, first Mem's bones will become flimsy, then her whole self will turn sheer, then transparent, then shadow, then vapor. She will become foggy air and then disperse, there will be no stopping it. She can already feel herself becoming less substantial, less thing-like, every second. She looks at her hand, expecting it to be partly translucent as a pair of dark stockings. But it isn't. It's just a hand, three-dimensional and opaque.

Then it comes, the sound they have been waiting for—a trio of sighs. Little puffs, snorts, and gasps begin to grow, like music at the beginning of a song when the voices haven't started. Mem looks down at the grass, the legs, the black shoes. She knows it is there, she can feel it.

Little lazy whore.

The skin under her skin grows thick, her eyes prickle around the edges.

No wonder your father left.

Her nose fills and swells. The wet in her mouth turns viscous. A tornado-shaped hunger pang burns behind her ribs. She doesn't notice that Derasha is watching her. She can't see anything beyond the luminous blur of almost-shed tears. She feels it coming, a symphony cresting—

Then the voices start. First Mem's mother.

Aunt Ayin.

Aunt Binah.

And then Derasha, who suddenly has the skin of Mem's upper arm twisted like taffy between her fingers. The pain jolts Mem out of her reverie. She turns to face Derasha who gracefully holds a black handkerchief to her mouth and begins, decorously, to sob.

Sofie's eyes look at Mem and say *Oh, no.*

Then there are mutters, moans, whimpers, wails. Achy, wet sounds kneaded from throats. Animal sounds. The real mourners are silent. Mem pulls her arm out of Derasha's grip but it is too late now, the pangs are gone, the tears receding. She squints her eyes tight, hoping she can squeeze the tears back out of them like juice from a lemon. She digs her thumbnail into her fingers. She has suddenly forgotten almost all of her Lessons and everything she has been told except *If you can't do it I will have to leave you behind.*

Just then a huge sound erupts through the weeping chorus, the sound of someone choking, or falling. The sound of things breaking. It takes a second for Mem to realize what it is, and then she knows.

This is the sound of her mother.

Oh lord! she chokes. *Oh Jesus why?*

This isn't fake crying. It is real, something is wrong. Someone is hurting her mother. The sobs are enormous, not even sobs but shapes of pain, magnificent, lush, bursting red bubbles. Mem wants to turn around to look but knows she can't. She watches, instead, as teardrops drip from the end of Derasha's elegant nose. The sounds behind the girls are coming to a crescendo, howls and sobs and quivering noises, but none as strong as Mem's mother's. Mem understands that eventually it is going to come to an end, if she doesn't start crying soon her mother will have to leave her. She shuts her eyes so tight she sees sparks flash against the red curtain of her eyelids. *Come on, come on!* She bites her lip so hard she tastes blood but that's all there is, just blood, no tears. No tears at all. Even her mouth is a waterless rubber. And suddenly it is too late.

The sounds around Mem are receding, dropping their moist notes, sliding away into sniffling noises.

There is some slight hyperventilation.

A throat clearing.

A little groan.

Soon the real mourners turn and, in a drowsy parade, begin to walk back down the hill, where the cars are waiting. Mem watches the high heels and loafers and cuffs and stockings move away, getting smaller and smaller as they go down the hill, attached to halting and slightly stooped bodies. The widow stays by the grave. She stares at the air, plucking at the material of her suit jacket over her chest as if her fingers might be able to break through the cloth, tear at the body, and grab at her heart, if only her hands were strong enough.

A *heart attack*. She wants to attack her heart.

She doesn't cry but she has lost all composure. She is decomposing.

One of the mourners puts a hand on the widow's shoulder. He tilts his head to the side and says, "We're so sorry you lost him."

Lost: as if the widow's hand had slipped away from her husband's fingers in a crowd at the mall and she can't find him. *Lost*: temporarily missing, like a misplaced toy. Not the right word, *lost*, which implies that her cold, chickeny husband might someday be found again, alive and well but frazzled at the *lost-and-found*.

Mem knows that she will now be lost, on purpose, by her mother. This has been the test, and she has failed because of Derasha, who is proudly walking down the hill toward her mother's station wagon. Mem knows she should say something, do something, feel something, but she can't. Her feet are nightmarishly stuck in the grass. She pinches the embroidered flowers on her dry handkerchief and waits.

Inside of her head Mem hears Aunt Ayin reciting the Lesson of Emptiness: *You cannot be empty and cry at the same time. Remember the story of Nistar, whose name means something you can't explain. There are hundreds of 15th-century paintings of Nistar hanging in the most prestigious museums in the world. In each of the paintings, Nistar stands removed, almost not-there, gently veiled, head bent forward but shoulders still proud. She was the first Wailer to train her daughters using images that made them sad. Like Nistar, you must fill yourself up with images to use but never reveal them. And if, god forbid, you should find yourself empty on the job and at a total loss, just watch the Master Wailer nearest to you and emulate.*

Mem finally turns to look at her mother, who is staring at the widow, and Mem feels what must be her own heart breaking. She wonders if this is the beginning of dying. She learned that the body dies slowly and unsystematically, like an old car, starting with the brain while the liver continues to pump bile, intestines still directing gasses from the meal before the last meal. Death, her mother has explained, is not so much a process as it is the sporadic shutting down of processes. Death does not happen, it is not a happening, it is the draining of a happening, as cold is simply the absence of heat. It is a dropped plate, a switch turned off, a wire cut. The sound of things ceasing, not of things absent.

It is impossible to be empty and cry at the same time. Just watch the Master Wailer nearest to you and emulate. Look at your mother.

Mem looks at her mother. Even with her swollen eyes and nose she is so beautiful she is like a bright light that hurts to look at. Mem looks at her anyway. She looks at her standing to the side of the grave canopy, in front of the other mothers who seem too pale, too dim, their features too small. Mem's mother glows, super-bright against the stiff blacks. The other mothers defer to her, heads bent just a little as they wait to listen to her deep voice.

Look at her again.

These other mothers know that Mem's mother is the Master. That she is special, chosen, a legend, a star. That her blacks are the best blacks and her wails are the best wails and her handkerchiefs are hand-embroidered with forget-me-not patterns handed down for hundreds of generations from ancient Rome. They know this and so does Mem. Mem looks at her mother and her love for her comes out and goes forward like a beacon that connects them, even though her mother seems far away and isn't looking at Mem at all.

Mem without her mother.

Mem feels her chest shudder and her face begin to cry.

She loves her mother so much it hurts, it is a hole that can never be filled. Her mother is as big as the air around them; Mem gasps the air in, pulls at her hem, pulls everything in through her mouth, turns it into sound and lets it purge out. *You cannot be empty and cry at the same time.* This isn't true, can't be true, Mem's emptiness is as large as her mother. If she could only have all of her mother. If she could only be enough for her mother to love. If only there were such thing as enough.

Mem looks at her mother but she is engrossed in conversation with the other mothers; she starts to step toward Mem but her head is turned while she finishes a sentence.

Your mother loves you. Mem's mother tells her this all the time, and Mem knows it is true. But she suspects what lies beneath this love: an unlove, just as strong. She sees it. She hears it. She feels it trying to get in.

Lazyfilthyliar

The idea of this unlove makes Mem panic, makes Mem sad, makes her wonder what horrible things she has done to deserve it. She looks down at the grass fringing the edges of her Mary Janes like a decorative border and knows with the everyday certainty and solidity of the grass and shoes that her mother's unlove will always be there. She shifts her shoes in the green fur of the grass.

Lazyfilthyliar

Her mother suddenly looks at Mem and Mem feels it. She raises her head in time to see her mother smile and mouth *I love you baby.* Mem's insides roil in a swamp of redness and humiliation. *Filthy liar. Lazy whore. Piece of shit.*

No wonder

No wonder

No wonder your father left.

Mem's mother smiles again and the swamp inside Mem gets hotter and surges. Irrepressible mudflows bring the red up to Mem eyes, nose, and mouth, her face becoming a ripe fruit bursting with acidy juice that can no longer be contained. Suddenly, without any of the pomp and prelude she has always imagined, Mem's whole self is split open and weeping.

At the moment when the mourners stop walking and turn to look at where the sound is coming from, Mem forgets how to breathe. She can only cry out. Nothing goes in. Where is her mother? She looks around, sobbing. The tears are made of boiled water and vinegar. They are too hot. They burn. They score Mem's cheeks with sickle-shaped scars.

There is no such thing as Mem without her mother.

They're going to bury Mem's mother, but not yet. Mem reaches out to touch the cool face bright with stardust but her fingers don't reach; they're already lowering the coffin. In the middle of this pinwheel of mourners, in the strange light on her slack face in the coffin, Mem's mother's corpse is suddenly beautiful, even her mouth beautiful, though Mem knows it is stitched closed and stuffed. The lips seem kissed by petals of moonlight, skin dusted with a fine, glowing powder, like the dust from moths' wings.

"Don't go!" shrieks Mem.

Her mother's coiled hair shines even brighter than the pink satin it rests upon. Her hands are folded over the belly. Mem sobs. Mem wails. Snot runs into her mouth.

"Don't go!"

It feels good to say it. It makes her cry harder. She says it again.

And again.

And again, rocking back and forth, the cloth of her doole stuffed between her pulling fingers.

"No!"

A handful of mourners clamber back up the hill and rush over to Mem, dropping things, falling onto knees to comfort her, to make her stop. They offer her handkerchiefs, candy, hugs. She twists away from them, turning around.

"No!"

And there is her mother. Smiling. Arms crossed. Watching, mouthing, *You are a good girl.*

Now Mem wants to stop but she doesn't know how. She's supposed to stop by making herself feel something else, by remembering something happy or funny or nice. Mem tries to feel something else but she can't. There is nothing else. There is only this. Small body crooked down, white ghost wrapped in black, warped spine contracting, pores flared, nostrils streaming. Mouth in the shape of pain.

This is the shape pain makes.

This is the prologue to heaving and screaming.

This is a picture of Mem weeping.

In her mind Mem hears Aunt Ayin reciting, *The desire of the weeping body is not to stand but to sit, not to sit but to lie, not to lie but to curl and contract, puckering like a sour mouth. The weeping body wants to recoil, withdraw, retreat. Don't do any of these things. Remember Adrastia, jailed in Rome in the 6th century B.C. for breaking Solon's law by crying in public. Remember how she refused to stop and wept so lavishly behind her bars that even the guards threw coins at her feet.*

Mem tries to straighten her body, to breathe normally again and let it all sink back down. She knows she is supposed to do it quickly, like her mother, in one brisk flick, the kind you use to check the undersides of leaves or the bottoms of bricks where beetles grow. The widow has covered her own mouth with her hand as she stares at Mem, and Mem is instantly overcome with embarrassment, as if she were standing here naked in front of all these people.

One of the mourners stands off to the side, waiting. He is an older man with white hair and a white mustache, wearing a tweed suit. A thin man with fat hands. Mem takes one look at him and knows he is the kind she's been warned about. There is usually at least one at every job, her mother explained, an older man who cranes his neck so he can watch the Wailers drip and snot, the smeared mascara, the opened mouths. The kind of man who makes *psst psst* noises at women and says rude things in languages that they do not understand. When Mem's mother was a teenager she had one man who followed her from job to job. Finally she called the police to complain. The policeman who answered the phone listened to Mem's mother explain and then interrupted. "Come on, lady, what do you expect?" he had asked. "I mean, look at what you do for a living, for Chrissakes."

Eventually, the man stopped showing up. But Mem's mother still keeps a watchful eye upon her audiences, looking for voyeuristic old men who are all too fascinated with what is going on behind them. Too often, she has noted, the most ardent observers are men of the cloth, straining over their hymn books during pauses to behold the moaning, the submission, the rare dripping of womanly fluids. A few times Mem's mother has caught the eye of some salivating minister and wagged her tongue at him, mid-sob.

The letchy-looking man in tweed walks over to Mem, smiling broadly. He claps his meaty hands.

"Bravo," he says. "What a wonderful job you did! Talented and love-ly, too, what a combination!"

Mem is embarrassed but she smiles, a small smile. When the man walks closer Mem sees that his skin is mottled with pocks and scars, the inside of his lopsided nostrils lined with a hard yellow crust. His eyes are moist, but not from crying.

"How much for you to cry for just me?" he asks, his rheumy eyes pink, cigar-shaped fingers stuttering over the wallet swelling out of his breast pocket. *Tap, tap, tap.*

"I'm not allowed," Mem says softly. "I'm sorry."

She smiles politely again. She doesn't want to offend him. She tries to fix her eyes on something else, the trash lining the street by the cemetery like unwanted food pushed to the side of a plate, the man's loose shirt but-ton dangling like a teddy bear's floppy eye. The man looks disappointed, but not defeated. He nods his head, tapping his wallet. "Okay, lovely," he says. "I understand." He takes Mem's hand and kisses the top of it and walks away.

After he is gone Mem can still feel his spit on her hand. She rubs it against the back of her doole. His fingers felt just the way they looked, fat sausages wrapped in dry leaves. Mem bends down and pulls up a handful of grass, using all of her fingers. She sprinkles the grass onto a nearby headstone, so that anyone looking might just think she is paying her respects in the traditional Jewish way. But that isn't why she does it. She just needs to get the feeling of the man off of her fingers, to touch some-thing else.

Mem looks at her hand, slowly turning it so that she can examine both sides. But there isn't anything else there. It's just a hand.

Aunt Ayin stands next to Sofie and watches. She tugs at the side seam of her doole and stretches her neck. She frowns and snorts, creasing her brow. She says, "Well, I guess Mem's a natural after all. *Kinaherah.*" But she is not pleased.

— 1896 A.D., MASSACHUSETTS, UNITED STATES —

ARCHIVAL EXCERPT

Developments in Theory, Technique and Training:
A Handbook of Three Approaches to Wailing
English text by Sergio James.
Ungar-Weekes Publishing Company.

ON DAILY INSTRUCTION

Daily exercises

It is earnestly recommended that the following exercises be dili-
gently studied every day, and with new transpositions. First slowly
and with a firm touch, and then faster. These include Syncopation,
The Hold or Pause, Cadence, The Trill, Modulation, Posture and
Movement, and Use of Props.

Faulty Habits

For the appalling effects of early negligence and inattention in
these matters is productive of much that is faulty and often very
difficult to correct. On this ground might be mentioned the sticking out of the elbows, the employ of clownish facial expressions,
and the lax positioning of the hands and fingers. Additional poor
habits reinforced by the unmindful and therefore neglectful
supervision of the trainer habitually include slurred notes or
erratic jumps through the octaves, usually caused by slipshod
comprehension of the Seven Primary Tones.

On the Importance of Perseverance

It is not without grave determination with which the young
apprentice must adhere to lessons both physical and historical,

regardless of the onset of any physical or psychic exhaustion that may develop. To succumb to such trifles during apprenticeship would be to indulge the malignant natures of laziness and ignorance, two dispositions characteristic of the lowest caste of wailing women. One must thus advance natural traits while concurrently acquiring new attributes, disregarding or suppressing any indolent urges through the studious exercise and repetition of daily lessons.

6

"Is it true your mother tortured you to teach you how to cry?"

While her mother cooks dinner to celebrate Mem's First Funeral, Mem stands by the row of basil plants on the windowsill in the foyer and strokes the warty leaves of the smallest basil plant. She cups her hands around its pot, inhales its greenness, deeply. She whispers softly into its leaves, "Now your name is Frank." The packed flannel-patterned luggage is still waiting by the door, sitting on the linoleum. The linoleum tile is all over the house, in the kitchen and all the bathrooms, the laundry room, the mud room; it had come newly laid with the newly built house, and Mem's mother scrubs every inch of it on her knees once a week. Through the foyer window Mem sees a group of children walking home from the bus stop, each carrying a piece of brightly colored construction paper shaped like a bird, a flower, a shoe, with wadded-up tissue paper glued on for details. Mem hears them laugh loudly, the rubbery bounce of their footsteps against the pavement. In the kitchen, Mem's mother sings to herself, clattering through the silverware drawer.

Mem and her mother have often used the great-grandmother's silver for romantic Friday night dinners. On these nights, Mem's mother cooks and plays a cassette of old jazz songs sung by women with grated voices. Sometimes Mem's mother sings along while she cooks. Sometimes they dance together, spinning around the kitchen, Mem's mother conducting an invisible band with a sauce-stained wooden spoon.

Mem wanders into the kitchen and sees the silver gleaming next to the plates and glasses like coins. Her mother is singing *I know you'll leave me someday soon* while she lights the candles. Mem makes flowers out of the thin paper napkins and places them gingerly inside the glasses. They take off their shoes and sit down to eat dinner barefooted, swinging their legs and laughing.

But there is a small, thin, hysterical wire vibrating inside of Mem that has never been there before. Mem wants to enjoy herself the way she usually does with her mother but now she isn't sure she can trust the good time she is having. Everything she says, every movement she makes with her body is followed by a silent question: *Is this right? Are you angry? Do you still love me?* When Mem's mother accidentally knocks the antique white porcelain salt cellar off the counter with her elbow, Mem flinches. It's a one-of-a-kind collector's item, hand-thrown in France, and as it falls it smashes quickly and completely, blasting a soft white halo of *fleur de sel* around the floor. Mem's mother bends breathlessly down to fish out the porcelain fragments and withdraws her hand, abruptly, as if burned. A little blood drops into the circle of salt on the floor. Her mother laughs and runs cold water over her fingers, then wraps her thumb in a kitchen towel patterned with strawberries. She shakes her hips and sings. *If you have to leave, I'll try not to mind, but please don't leave my heart behind...*

The blood does not bother Mem. It means that her mother's body is alive, beating, with blood still in it. They leave the salt, light the candles, and drink apple juice out of large wine glasses so big that most of Mem's face can fit past the rim. They make toasts to Aurora and toasts to Billie Holiday and finally a toast for Mem's First Funeral. "To my beautiful girl," Mem's mother says, leaning over the plates of pasta. They make their glasses kiss by touching them together.

"Do you know what we're celebrating?" asks her mother in between bites. The pasta twirls around their heavy forks like yarn.

"My First Funeral?" says Mem, unsure. The candlelight dazzles her eyes, making everything glossy and watery. Mem's mother is haloed with energy and light. Suddenly, Mem's love for her mother assaults her small body, without warning and immense, opening its many arms like flowers, filling up the room and bursting through the glass of the windows, its vines and fruits warm and thick as blood and older than Mem's mother will ever be. Mem knows she will never be strong enough for this love that now fills and overfills her like an ocean unfurling its waves into a thimble.

Her mother looks up from her pasta wearing her smiling someone-else face and says, "What are you staring at, you piece of shit."

All of the blood in Mem's body rushes up under the surface of her skin as her stomach drops. Her mother takes a sip from the big glass. She leans over the table toward Mem and gently strokes Mem's chin with her fingertips. "Well," she says, "you've wasted the last six years of my life, that's for sure." She leans in closer, her hair almost in Mem's plate, and whispers, "You didn't even try, you lazy fucking whore."

"I'm sorry," says Mem, but her voice doesn't sound at all like her own voice. It sounds like a mouse, if a mouse could talk.

Mem's mother says, quietly, "You have humiliated me and insulted all of the women of our line."

"I'm sorry," Mem squeaks again.

"You're sorry? You're sorry!" screams Mem's mother. "I'm sorry I ever had you!"

Mem's mother's body jolts around the table so that it's directly in front of Mem. She is so close that Mem can see all the pores on her nose, she can smell the smoky smell of her mother's hair.

"You're lazy, Mem."

Mem looks down at her feet.

"I did try," she says, sounding like a mouse again.

"You're lazy and now you're a liar, too."

Mem shakes her head.

"I'm not lying," squeaks Mem, but it sounds like a lie. It feels like a lie. Her whole self is a lie. "I did try."

"'I'm not lying,'" squeaks Mem's mother, pulling a false-sad face. "'I did try.'"

Here comes the red.

Blood red.

Pomegranate red.

Not-the-color-of-love red.

Mem's mother opens her mouth and screams at Mem *liar liar liar lazy filthy fucking liar* so loud that little pieces of spit fly out of her mouth and onto Mem's surprised and flinching face.

You always fuck everything up, you dirty whore. I wish I never had you. Stupid little shit.

Then something comes out of Mem.

It starts in her bowels and rushes up, up, up, out of her eyes and nose and mouth all at once, big and wet and red, and she can't stop it. It makes her lungs jerk and sounds even worse than the squeaking. She can't breathe in or close her mouth, but somehow this is worse than the weeping at the funeral. Later in life Mem will remember these episodes with her mother as the moments when saliva thickens and tear ducts bleed, the salt and the water pouring from their secret source. The source of her own mouth opening, the hole of her mouth, the bare mouth growing to let something out. She will remember what can't be released. She will remember the color red.

Mem's mother loosens her face so that it is smooth again, Mem's mother's real face, open and level and calm, a deep pond on a windless day. She wraps her arms around Mem and holds her tight.

She coos, "Good girl. Good girl. That's my good girl. Oh, I'm so proud of you." She bundles Mem up against her breasts and rocks her back and forth and strokes her hair. Mem tries to breathe but the jerking won't go away. She tries to pretend she is being loved by her mother.

"See? You are a natural."

The weeping is fading, but only on the outside. It slithers back down inside of her with its teeth clenched around *lazyfilthyliar*. Mem is sticky, her nose huge and bulbous as Frank's. She can feel every crease on her body.

"Shh, my good girl. I love you so much. You have perfect pitch, you sound like a dream."

Mem can hardly hear anything but her heart attacking, her own blood pounding against her cranium, and the creak of her mother's shoulders turning in their sockets as she rocks Mem back and forth, back and forth.

"It is all that honey I put in your formula when you were an infant," she whispers into Mem's hair. "You wouldn't take any formula, so I had to sweeten it. Now you're too sweet."

Mem closes her eyes and the salt from her tears turn into crystals that grow legs, like mites.

Her mother whispers, "I should have used salt."

The mites cover Mem's whole face, moving down her body, nibbling till there is nothing left but a white pile of bone-dust and a white pile of salt and with one good gust they are both blown away by the wind.

"I'm so proud of you," Mem's mother whispers. "So proud. Do you know your eyes are a thousand times more beautiful when you're crying?"

Mem's feet dangle beneath the table while her hot, smothered breath spreads itself against her mother's arms.

Mem hears her mother's mouth say, *I love you.*

Plain mouth. Easy mouth.

You are the greatest thing I have ever done.

I am so proud of you.

I love you.

"I love you," says her mother's mouth, covering Mem's forehead with kisses. "I love you."

She gently turns Mem's face up toward her own and this time what Mem sees is an anxious pleading. Her mother whispers, "Do you love me?" And Mem nods, furiously, unable to answer out loud. Mem knows her mother is her only link to the rest of the world, a channel through which Mem must perceive and receive all things. Mem's mother is an irresistible force, massive and compact, a spoonful of dead star that no one can lift. She is like this because she loves Mem. It is this love which occupies Mem's mother's self so enormously, dense and magnetic and purring with heat. It is the love which makes the molecules collapse in her wake, burning around her a halo of friction. This is why people so often need to open the windows when Mem's mother is in the room, even on days when it snows. It is because she loves Mem.

"Mem, do you love me? I don't believe that you really love me."

Of course Mem loves her mother. But Mem's love is different. It is not so huge. It is long and coiled instead, sprung tight through each vessel, edged with a million small teeth and anchored in the bones. Mem's love is incessant, corkscrewed, metallic. It won't stretch or soften. It aches when she moves.

— 1990 A.D., PENNSYLVANIA, UNITED STATES —

Leah Kang, Arcadia University

A Violation of Decency and Good Taste:
Approaches to the Anthropological Study of Weeping Women

> She hade a charming colour, eies bryt, all flowring mouthe, and
> so wet with pane, but howe depraved the tratoress, against god
> and naiture...the slatterne is an insirection, a vyle difeilment of
> all things desent and divein...Repente! Repente! Repente!
> —Sir Richard J. Lorrie, 1554 Reformer of British legislation
> concerning wailing women

While this thesis strives to catalogue and connect the scant available evidence of the history of an endangered culture, we must remember that most of our limited sources were once little more than objects of art or decoration. Because so much of what we can use may have only served as fanciful invention, our interpretations are largely dependent upon the ways artists and writers perceived, interpreted, and represented wailing women of their time and country. Heightening our challenge, weeping women throughout the centuries have been taught to deliberately "leave no trace," and—under pain of exclusion and the disgrace of their entire matriarchal blood-line— were forbidden to reveal details of apprenticeship, career, or ancestral history to any individuals unaffiliated with the trade. (*At Your Disposal,* Alfreds and Troll 1994) Because of this, while we have discovered a few historical fragments related to wailing, no one has encountered a complete first-hand account as of yet.[1] Available secondhand accounts are less than kind, unfavorably characterizing wailing women as lawless hysterics, depraved criminals, and women of easy virtue.[2]

These accounts, many discovered by Dr. Holly P. Gentile (author of *Decay and Decadence: Essays on the Necrotic Arts and the Anatomy of Wailing* 1987), make up the bulk of our paltry anthropological canon. The most significant of these are excerpts from a group of thirty-seven letters written by turn-of-the-century male British explorers, almost all rife with vivid reports of having witnessed exotic acts of native professional mourning.[3] These included vividly detailed accounts of indigenous wailing women who, the authors claimed, were considered "worse than whores" by their own cultures. This particular assessment appears to have been a common comparison held throughout the ages. In fact, the very European royals who had hired thousands of professional mourners to attend aristocratic family funerals were the same sophisticated elements in society who regularly referred to Wailers as "slatternly thieves and common whores of the most degrading kind," and "the most disgusting kind of woman to be likened only...to a whore." (Gentile 1983)

In *The Sin Against Water*, Louise Casey (1976) maintains that this judgment (leaking from the eyes in public being a greater sin than exposing one's genitals to a stranger in private) was so often implied because, like "whores," wailing women performed physical, submissive, and degrading acts for money and were required to create lives that were both noble and shameful in order to provide a secret service relegated to their sex. Casey also argues that, historically, males have felt a general sense of unease about the existence of any clan of women who—by "virtue" of their unmarried status—have never had to submit to traditional male/female domestic politics. Scottish sociologist Kira Mathews, however, suggests that weeping women have been reviled in response to an enduring male

---

1. Ironically, wailing women were among the first women in the world to learn how to read and write, though they were rarely permitted to do either in public.

2. While Troll explains that the very existence of weeping women was believed to be "beyond a threat to decency...a parasitic social evil governed by harlots determined to undermine and obliterate civilized values," (1994) she fails to mention that some members of the same societies were secretly enamored with the women, evidenced by odes and letters found in France, Italy, Poland, and the United States.

3. The letters are abundant with descriptions of "alien" cultural death customs, including weeping women being paid to strangle the widows, poison the dogs, wear hair, amputate digits, mutilate their flesh, wash or not wash, whiten or blacken their bodies, and take part in cannibalism.

paranoia about women exerting political influence from behind the scenes. Classically, Mathews asserts, the role of the woman as witness and emotional translator of grief has been mostly universal, and thus often interpreted as a perpetual threat to ruling patriarchal authorities. Mourning was one of the only forms of acceptable public expression and power available to women in ancient Greece. Beginning in the 6th century BC, a series of laws was passed limiting public lamentation and condemning the purchase of wailing women in order to suppress the possible insubordinate power of women's mourning and limit ostentatious displays by the state's wealthier citizens.[4] (Hamilton 1955) These forms of prohibition resurface throughout the century (note Sophocles' Greek heroine Antigone's death during her imprisonment for mourning in public) and can still be found in modern American legislation. (Mathews 1997)

However, Mathews is careful not to relate why such unsparing slander and defamation have managed to follow wailing women across the globe and throughout generations. The training techniques used by mothers to coach young would-be wailing women (including the fondling of corpses, extreme physical and emotional abuse, illegal home-schooling, the fanatical worship of Roman goddesses) have been cited as the primary cause for centuries of legislative attention and persecution. (Gentile 1983) The constant threat of abandonment is key here, since a novice must be "sent away or left behind" if she cannot perform by age seven. Paradoxically, a daughter is obliged to abandon her mother if she (the mother) becomes permanently unable to perform before the age of 60, an intriguing reversal of which we have no account. (Mathews 1997)

Little attention has been paid to the obvious difficulties such cultural estrangement must present for any young girls still training in the United States, as it is also forbidden for Wailers of any age to enjoy modern enter-

---

4. This may perhaps be influenced by a specific period's relationship between mourning and vengeance, as well as the recognition of role fulfillment and the weeper-widow transaction as proof of high emotional investment.

tainments (such as television or pop music), or indulge in outside intellec-
tual pursuits (Jeffreys and Marc 1998); much like the anachronistic lives of
Pennsylvania Dutch youth or a first American-born Asian child raised
with a foreign value system in the home, an apprenticing weeping woman
must learn to manage living within two extremely different cultures.
Unlike most traditional customs which demand that participants either celebrate, renounce, or endure, the young wailing woman has little recourse
but to cooperate; no matter how persuasive the pull of modern culture may
be, it lacks the one dominant element which works to keep a Wailer "in her
place": her omnipotent mother. The mother-loyalty cultivated through
weeping women's rearing is apparently so pervasive that we have yet to
find an artifact or modern tale describing a daughter's defection from the
sect (*ibid*). In *Aurora's Pose*, J. Mitchell suggests that young weeping
women are keenly aware of the ways in which their upbringing has
ensured that they will simply not be capable of surviving in the "unprofessional world." (1999) They possess no legal names, have no human con-
tacts outside of the industry, are not lawfully educated, and have not developed any professional skills with which to make a legitimate living.[5]
Additionally, as explained by Donall O'Roberts in *Studies in the Theory of
Lachrymal Response* (1992), while the current trends in entertainment have
blurred the lines between private and public, our culture has continued to
support an institutionalized sense of shame surrounding public displays of
almost any demonstrative emotion.[6]

In his ground-breaking essay, *What Remains: The Case of the Last
Professional Mourner* (1996), Philip A. David holds that almost all of the
wailing families still in existence in the United States arrived during a

---

5. The double-naming is typical of many groups living on the fringe of society; wailing women's
secret names come from specific lessons found in the kabala.

6. Unless the demonstrator is being paid exorbitant amount of money to do so on film. There
are other exceptions: weddings, births, deaths and war still seem to be fundamentally accepted
situations where the exhibition of emotion is tolerable, providing that it is not overdone.

Wailer's Purge in 1903; wailing women from Italy, Spain, and Greece had been run out of Europe and soon settled in a new land where mourning was considered "a private and oft embarrassing affair." Like all cultures that employ ancestry as a method of caste system, there is still much debate addressing the issue of lineage. Although most wailing women will, quite vehemently, declare that their ancestors hail from either Rome or Greece beginning around 1200 B.C., recently recovered artifacts reveal that Wailers were usually a mixed, bilingual breed perpetually vacillating between the two empires, depending upon legislative fashion, cultural trends, and wealth of the area. Their shared reverence and idolization of the Roman goddess Aurora support this finding. (Mitchell 1999) Cheri Elphmenn (*Perspectives of Public Mourning Throughout the Ages*, 1988) maintains that while death laws and fashions seem to change as rapidly as societies transform, the one aspect of human nature which has managed to remain constant since ancient Greco-Roman times is simply that we like to watch. This, Elphmenn suggests, is perhaps why history's weeping women often come across more like today's actresses than yesterday's "whores." [7,8]

In her landmark article, *In Defense of Wailers* (1968), Ella Dylan reports that when the necrotic arts were still in vogue in England (up until the 1820s), popular customs of the time included engraved funeral invitations, the wearing of corpses' hair as clothes—often referred to as weeds or blacks—and the distribution of dozens of mourning gowns, scarves, or cloaks to people unknown to the dead so as to make it appear that the deceased was popular with the masses. Dylan explains that these garments were known as "doole," (derived from the Latin doleo, meaning *I grieve*).

---

7. I find interesting that until recently, the station of an actress was also considered less than or equal to that of a whore. In Reclaiming Our Truth (1979), Robin Lawrence asks, "Are there any jobs, historically, for women, where we are not compared to whores? Will whores forever be the yardstick by which all of our behaviors and career choices and levels of craft are measured?"

8. It is worth noting that—although there have been great recent achievements in the science of sound and its refinement—there are no audio-tapes of these women in existence.

An unprecedented 900 black gowns were distributed at the funeral of the
Earl of Oxford—200 given to weeping women along with their fees. Many
aristocrats kept well-preserved collections of their dooles as souvenirs.
When the funeral processions had come to an end, however, it was not
unusual to see wailing women by the dozens "rounded up" by local
authorities, while cautionary tracts condemning the "wretched souls"
were distributed, declaring that the women in question were appalling,
prideful, and impure (*ibid*).

There were exceptions; in a letter written June 6, 1401, Marquis Jean S.
Cainlon, a high-ranking Parisian judicial official, pleaded with a "weeping
maid" to admit and then disown her heritage so that he might be able to
legally absolve her: "It is because I love you earnestly for your integrity
and kindness, I have urged you to remedy your apparent oversight, or
excessive determination which has emerged in you, a weeping maid pas-
sionate in this issue, out of conjecture or pride…I plead, instruct and
demand you…please put right, withdraw and rectify your aforesaid
error…acknowledge your mistake, and we will have mercy, and will offer
you favorable reparations." (Hamilton 1955)

7

"Were you allowed to play like a normal child?"

The day after her First Funeral, Mem spends the afternoon in the backyard, watching the inconsolable wasps stumble around the sticky spots on the wood picnic table. The wasps are tired, shriveled up like old grapes in the soupy late-August haze. They know they are going to die soon. They mistake bottles for flowers and sputter like cars out of tune. The sky is lidded by a solid drape of cloud as sultry as the seamy skin that floats to the top of boiling milk. Mem can smell the backs of her knees as she and Sofie sit on their haunches, using spoons to dig through the dehydrated patchwork quilt of grass and dirt. Her hands sweat brownly.

In a few days Mem will work her second job. Mem is relieved to have been left at home, and happy to be digging with spoons in the backyard, despite the heat, despite the fact that the inside of the house is shivery and brisk with central air-conditioning. She prefers to be outside and likes the smell of the dirt, the muffled buzz of conditioning compressors vibrating the summer air, the sound of the spoons sifting small stones and soil.

The spoon ends are shaped like flat roses, black from age along the edges, part of a set their Uncle Irv stole from the Ritz Carlton when he was a young bellhop, just two months before he was shot by a sniper on the beach during the war. Those were days when people still died of vague-sounding things like *consumption* and *squalor*. When people *perished*, instead of passing away. Irv's sister Bella, Mem and Sofie's great-aunt, had been a suffragette working in a cigar factory for extra money at the time. The day young Irv came home with his pockets full of spoons he found that his sister had been taken to a hospital to have her reproductive organs removed—to cure her of *questionable* and *promiscuous* behavior. From that day on Bella could do nothing but cry. No more wrapping big leaves into cigars. No more rallying with shouts and signs. Soon after, she became the most talented Wailer in the state. This was a sad story with a good ending, told over and over again to remind Mem and Sofie that although bad things happening might not make you stronger, they can always make you money.

Every time Mem looks at the spoons with *Ritz Carlton* engraved in cursive on the back she pictures her great-aunt having a grand old time in the factory, smiling and laughing and swinging her high-heeled feet as she makes cigars and puts them into neat wooden boxes. In Mem's imagination her great-aunt has tumbling dark hair and straight, white teeth, the best smile in the factory. But the word *suffragette* contradicts this image. It sounds like a fancy title for a professional mourner, the name of a girl who likes to suffer.

Mem has just learned that her mother's secret name, *Celeste*, came from the Celestial Waters, the enduring and the saving waters, the sun and moon dissolved and united like water and salt. When Mem was very little, her mother had a small side business using salt for clients requesting more "mystical" services. She would drop a pinch of sacred salt (from Shoprite) onto a scroll of hallowed bark (from the backyard) and read the scatterings like tea leaves. She would hunch over the bark, scratching her chin and staring at the sprinkling of crystals like an astronomer studying constellation maps, a miniature galaxy done to scale. *A prosperous year. Sudden illness. Good domestic luck.* Cynicism laced her voice as she said these things, believing them and not believing them, happy to take the money from those who would rather believe. *The salt is wise. Where are you broken? It cures. It heals. It preserves.*

It makes everything okay.

Sofie is named for *Ein Soph*, a hidden place of forgetting and oblivion.

A place not on Earth, not in the world of limited things. *Ayin*, for the wisdom of nothingness, anything sealed and concealed. By the rest of the world they are called Isabella and Anne, names that mean nothing.

Isabella. Mem looks at Sofie sweating and knows this is the wrong name for her.

They work industriously, not saying much to one another, planting as many rows of salt as possible in the small yard. Soon Sofie's round face is sheened with sweat and grit, her secondhand Mickey Mouse baseball shirt soaking through. Mem can see where perspiration is collecting, dripping from between Sofie's small rolls.

Mem is sweating, too. The parched clots of earth are hard to scoop out. Some spots are full of pebbles. But Mem doesn't care. She knows the salt garden will take some time. *It will be worth it in the end*, Mem reminds herself as she pushes her sweaty palms against the flat roses. Soon there will be fields of frosted pebbles of salt blooming in glowing and white buds like kernels of corn. Salt clustered on vines. Brittle icicle leaves shining like slices of mica. On one side there will be a row of salt trees, and when these blossom Mem will beat the trees with sticks and get showered with salt instead of olives, catching it in buckets like snow that will never melt. When the wind blows the salt fields will chime like good crystal rubbed with wet fingers and when the rain rattles the trees the salt garden will sparkle like raindrops on a spider web. The vines will twinkle in the moonlight and Mem will pretend she is playing in a playground of stars.

Maybe Aurora will get confused and think Mem's salt fields are the heavens. Maybe Mem will find her there, luminous as the ringing salt rows, lost between the bulging salt bulbs and white flowers. Maybe Mem's mother will be proud when she sees the garden, happy for the chance to meet Aurora. They can sell the salt and be rich and never have to weep again. No more looking at Mem as if she is something her mother has picked out from between her teeth to inspect. No more people watching. No more pretend.

"Let's pretend we're dead," Sofie says, putting her spoon down. Her hair sticks to her sweaty forehead and when she pushes it away her fingers leave a smear of dirt. "Let's play Funeral."

Mem looks down at the hole she is digging and pokes her spoon at it. There is dirt and salt under her fingernails. She shrugs.

Sofie instantly brightens. "Okay," she says, hurriedly. "Then you can be the deceased." Mem shrugs again and settles down in the yellow grass. It crisps and crunches against her back, scratching her scalp.

Sofie clears her throat, puts her spoon down, bends over, and covers her face with her hands.

"Oh Mirabelle! Why did you die!" she moans. "Why oh why oh why Mirabelle!"

Mem opens one eye and sees Sofie pretending to pull at her hair and clothes as she wails.

"Hey!" says Mem. "You're not even weeping!"

Sofie rolls her eyes like Derasha. "I'm just practicing, silly. Doesn't your mother practice before the funerals?"

"No," said Mem. "It's unprofessional…it's not authentic."

"That's not true. Your mother doesn't know anything."

"You don't even know what authentic means, do you?" Mem teases. "And why do you keep calling me Mirabelle? That's stupid. You know my name."

Sofie rolls her eyes again and sighs impatiently.

"Because," she explains crossly. "This is a *job*. In *public*. I can't call you Mem in public, you know."

"But if this is a funeral, it means I'm dead and all that doesn't matter anymore," says Mem.

"It will matter even more because when you die you take your secret name with you so God knows who you are and lets you into heaven," said Sofie, adding, "Stupid."

Mem looks disgustedly at Sofie. "Don't call me stupid," she says, but she is suddenly too hot to argue.

Sofie's voice changes. "If I died for real," she asks, "would you be sad?"

Mem nods solemnly. She says, "I would be so sad they wouldn't even have to pay me to cry."

They play Funeral until the sun sets, with Mem as the deceased every time. With her eyes closed she sees white. Arctic white. The alien white of the Mansion of the Moon Aunt Ayin is always talking about. Mem sees the white of this mansion, a place the sun forgot, howling echoes grinding their way against voluptuous drifts and peaks of dry snow. The wind drags its colossal fingers across a pyramid of ice, sculpting milk-glass windows and mansion doors, alabaster columns and a backyard fence. There Mem sits under a parasol of pure white leaves while the shadows cast heavenly designs on the powdery ground like candle-lit lace.

But she can hear the fathers back on Earth opening screen doors and storm doors and patio doors, their barbecue tools clanging dully together like cowbells. She knows that in a minute she will hear the sound of fires starting. She will smell briquettes and coal and overdoses of lighter fluid. In a minute she will have to come back from her mansion and go inside the house where her own father isn't.

With her eyes closed, Mem imagines, in slow and painstaking detail, how she has died. In the first death Mem has accidentally shot herself with her own arrow. The sensation of the arrow striking her chest feels like a massive bee sting. Next Mem is murdered by an angry mob brandishing the necessary pitchforks and torches and an indecipherable orchestra of shouts. Then Mem's heart simply stops while she is eating breakfast. It takes her until she has scraped up the last spoonful of cereal into her mouth to realize she is dead. Later she is slain by a spurned lover and dies of a broken heart, clutching a handkerchief to her forehead for dramatic pause.

In the final death, Mem is at a wedding where she dances so well and so fast that her bare feet catch fire, burning her alive.

When the coroner comes to make his report he writes, *death by dancing*.

That night, when she returns from work, Mem's mother stacks several packed suitcases where the one suitcase used to sit alone. She stands by the luggage and leans against the wall. "If you don't do it right the next time I'll have to go," she says, peeling flakes of dark polish off her nails. "If you say you can do it and then you don't, you'll be a liar, and I don't like liars, so I'll leave." She walks slowly into the kitchen to begin cooking dinner.

Mem sneaks out back to check her salt holes. The night sky is fisheye-curved, round and violet. Feeble points of light shine through the purple dome like holes in a sieve. *You know the stars are made of secrets, that's why they shine like that*, Aunt Ayin once said. *They're God's secrets peeking through his old dark garments. If he took off his cloak we would all be blinded, like Solomon.*

Isn't Solomon the one who was blinded by his own tears? Mem had asked.

No, that was St. Francis of Assisi, said Aunt Ayin. *He cried till he went blind. But that's impossible, you know.*

The grass is thirsty, yellow-crisped, it crunches under her bare feet, spiking between her toes. Mem can make out the perimeter of her salt garden, the carefully dug rows of holes with plenty of space in between so the salt plants have room to grow. She bends down to take a closer look and for a second something around the holes sparkles. A quick glitter, then it is gone.

In the morning, Mem looks again and sees the morning dew in her backyard. She sees that Aurora's tears are not shaped like tears, they are too round, clustering clear pearls suspended from grass blades and awnings. There is an unreal perfection in her tears, a glimmering spectacle displayed like a jeweler's window and curtained by a pretty cowl of mist in exactly the right shade of white. Mem realizes that Aurora is just another Wailer with a job to do, and like all those who mourn for a living, her tears are false, masquerading as grief.

But, unlike the rest who mourn for a living, Aurora is immortal. She has had ten thousand lifetimes to rehearse her weeping, to adjust her damp skirt-hems so they barely brush against the tops of trees, to practice the tilt of her head so the tears run in perfect paths down her face like snowmelt. She has clarified the image of her son dying so it is sharp and three-dimensional and almost crystal-bright. She pulls at her cords till the curtain is drawn and the sun opens (the smell of him, his favorite food) and the little clouds roll against the sky like lost marbles (his smile, his hands, the dandelion bouquets) and then there it is big and wet and red, coming out of her eyes and nose and mouth and all at once (the small dirt, his cough, the tattered baby blanket he would not relinquish) and it is awful, awful but she rides it, and when the time is right Aurora knows how to stop it, too.

This is the trick, Mem knows, the hard part, not the crying but the stopping. The abrupt putting away of things. Folding and repacking the secrets like her dead son's clothes. Closing up her face so that it is white and still as an undisturbed snow. Aurora is able to do it each day, she knows her waters will make their way, plummeting through faucets and wells and the stiff veins of plants.

Mem gets down onto her knees to look at her salt plants and sees a few flecks of mica glinting in the dirt. But there is nothing else. No smooth white leaves or blazing branches. No crystalline saplings with moon-colored fruits.

Just dirt.

Just rocks.

And lots and lots of holes.

That afternoon Mem and her mother work a funeral in a small cemetery not far from their house. Across the street from the plot, workers are demolishing a commercial building that has been, through the years, a deli, a shoe store, a pet shop, a bar, each expensively renovated before opening and each failing within a year. The rubble falls with a soft thundering noise but doesn't distract Mem from her job. She keeps picturing the empty holes in the backyard, the hole where her own mother's casket will someday be buried, the stack of luggage piled at the front door.

Mem without her mother.

Before it is even time to start, Mem's mouth is open and wailing. The real mourners, the priest, and the daughter of the deceased all crane their necks slightly so that they can hear her performance over the powdery thwacks and grinds coming from the other side of the street.

Behind her, Mem's mother begins to weep, too, but Mem barely hears it. The holes she pictures in her mind are growing, her mother's corpse fading inside the holes, the no-thingness of the holes, the nothing where there once was something, scoops of nothingness defined only by the somethingness around it. You can only tell that a hole is there by what is left behind. *Mem without her mother.* Mem is the thing that will be left behind. She begins to sob so hard she shudders, she cannot breathe out, she tries but the holes inside of her will not stop growing, sucking in the air, burning on the wick of the same desire, that first instinct she always has when she sees a hole: the urge to fill it up.

Mem fills her hands with her face.

Don't cover your face, you have to feel exposed. She hears the Lessons chiming in her ears and drags her hands back down. *If you are crying they cannot ignore you. If you are crying they cannot really see you. Your tears make you disappear. They make the world disappear. They are all the power of water and salt mines. They paint as they roll and shine in the dark. If you are crying, they can always find you. And since the inside of the mouth is always wet, after dawn and daybreak are gone, they might watch the first morning sun drink up your tears but still taste them drumming in their mouths.*

— 1988 A.D., PENNSYLVANIA, UNITED STATES —

LOWER BUCKS COUNTY WEEKLY CRIER

Grave Danger:
Shocking News That Could Save a Child—and Your Bank Account
by Judah M. Baer

Dirty money. Child abuse.
Subversive gangs.

No way any of that could be going on here, in Bucks County, right? After all, these are just the ills Philadelphia natives hoped to leave behind when they moved out of the city to Bucks County, a migration that helped to drop urban Philadelphia's population from 2.5 million to 1.3 million in less than ten years.

But there is something happening in our community that is just as corrupt as anything you'd expect to encounter in Philly. It's a horror most of us don't even know is taking place, even though it could be happening right now in the house next door. And—according to local authorities—it's a phenomenon that needs to be stopped.

Something To Cry About

According to Bensalem Township's Lt. S.R. Loccke, dozens of local little girls are being forced to live their lives as part of a nationwide underground cult, suffering serious physical and emotional abuse and being made to perform humiliating rituals in front of strangers for money. "Some of us have seen these girls crying at funerals, without anyone sus-

pecting they have been brainwashed by their mothers to be able to cry instantaneously," she said, adding that most folks would be surprised to discover how many unsuspected members of this sisterhood live among us, shopping at the local supermarket, chatting with neighbors at the post office, or baking cupcakes for cluster fundraisers.

The case of "Mirabelle," the little girl whose local performances have brought hundreds of phone calls into precincts throughout the Delaware Valley, continues to baffle local police. Although the precinct following her case doesn't have any photographs of the girl on file, everyone who has called to make a report has been able to recall her appearance in great detail: small, about 4'11", and thin, pale, with enormous dark eyes and black hair grown down past her waist. One testimonial described her as "very pretty but like she would break into a million pieces if you touched her." Another says that she seemed "like she had hollow...bird bones" and that her eyes looked like "the eyes of those starving kids on TV." Police have been unable to determine where the girl lives or what her legal name might be.

As part of a three-part series, we will be uncovering the truth about girls like Mirabelle, as well as unsuspecting victims in your area who have been bilked out of hundreds of dollars while suffering the new loss of a loved one.

Playing the Black Market

One such victim, a forty-nine-year-old Bridesburg resident and recent widow, explained that she was in a "weak and grief-stricken" state of mind when she was accosted in her own home by a tall, strikingly pretty woman in her thirties. The widow felt so pressured to properly memorialize her husband, she added, that it didn't dawn on her that she was being taken for a ride until weeks after her husband's funeral.

"At the time, I thought I was doing the right thing," explained the widow, who has asked to remain anonymous to protect her family. "She [the woman] came into my house three days after my husband died and she...told me that she was there to help me through a difficult time. She was very nice and seemed to understand how I was feeling, so I hired her." After making preliminary arrangements (the woman refused to provide a phone number or address), the widow paid the Wailer $200 in cash as a down-payment for her services. "I remember thinking, 'Wait a minute, is this even legal?' But she seemed very calm and...assured, so I thought it was okay."

It was a thought she would soon regret. At her husband's grave less than a week later, she saw the Wailer she had hired waiting to perform, along with a young, emaciated girl about eight years old. "At first I was shocked," she recalled. "On top of it being a school day, I mean, why would someone bring a child to this kind of thing?"

Again, the widow was too over-whelmed to question what was happening. Beleaguered by her own sadness, it took her a while before she realized that the woman she had hired—and the little girl—had started to perform. The sound they made together was so distressing during the lowering of the casket, she noted, that many of the mourners turned around to see what was going on. "People couldn't stop staring at the little girl. It was amazing...people who weren't even that close to [the deceased] started crying and some...people kept going over to her, one man even kneeled down on the wet grass to try to make her stop. It was like she put a spell on everyone there."

Now, she says, she realizes that the tall brunette must have been the little girl's mother, a thought that still keeps her up at night. "What kind of mother would make her daughter do such a thing? It still gives me the creeps."

Getting Stiffed

Once the service itself was over, the brunette approached the widow to collect the rest of her fee. The widow admits that plenty of the attendees had

seemed genuinely moved by the performance and made a point of compli-
menting the woman and child before
leaving the cemetery. Some even asked
for her hiring information.

But once all of the other mourners
were gone, the widow recalls, the woman
made her move, telling the widow that
the balance owed was three hundred dollars for her services and an additional
three hundred for the girl. "I couldn't
believe it!" Smith said. "Nobody asked
for her daughter to come. It was like she
[the mother] was forcing me to pay for
something I didn't want."

Too late, Smith realized that she had
gotten herself involved in something
that was illegal as well as immoral. "My
mother used those women at my father's
funeral, and one of my cousins had hired
three or four of them for her son's burial,
so it never occurred to me that it was
against the law," said the widow. "I knew
I had to pay her what she was asking but
I wished there had been somewhere I
could call to complain."

Now there is.

Spare the Sob Story
Last week, State Representative
Anthony J. DePaul, Jr. (R-10th), pushed
legislation through the House just days
after the appointment of former State
Revenue Secretary Ronda J. Daniels to
head Pennsylvania's Death Industry
Task-Force. The new directive, slated to
go into effect early January, will expand

current laws prohibiting the hiring of
professional mourners for funerals or
any other public display of mourning
deemed "obscene...or designed to produce an illegal audience," overriding
Democratic complaints that Republicans
were exploiting an emotionally loaded
issue in order to gain election-year
advantage. Analyst Isshaihah D. Walker
has been following develop-
(Continued on page 13A)

8

"How old were you when you became a star?"

The first article comes out on the day of Mem's eighth birthday. Mem's mother says that it is the best possible publicity, but she is concerned that the police might start watching and figure out who they are. She is *kvelling* with pride for Mem but tells her to not take any of the newspaper articles too seriously. She reminds Mem that eventually, stories on paper will be all that survive humanity, and soon after that all the water will be gone, and then the Earth, and the sun, and every scrap of documentation that any people were ever here, all the silly scribbling and cave paintings and film, and even the books, and the memory of books, because all roads lead to death and extinction. But the newspaper articles are at the very least proof that Mem has done the right thing, they are something she can touch and hold onto, something that might be able to keep her mother from going away.

Mem doesn't like the attention, doesn't like to be watched, but she loves knowing that hundreds of people a week gather round to hear the new prodigy cry. She loves watching her mother smile, loves the sound of the phone ringing to request her services. She feels, at those moments, beloved. All she has to do to make it happen is close her eyes and there is her mother's dead face, phosphorescent against the white satin, already part-ghost. The mourners file by her casket like a production line of sad, dutiful factory workers. Then there it is, the tingling in the nose, prickling behind the lids, and Mem doubles up, her sobs like the sound of an engine that won't turn over. She heaves in rhythm until all of her insides are out. She won't be surprised if she opens her eyes one day and sees her intestines dangling out of her mouth.

Already, Mem has her own calendar book to schedule her engagements. She has already been asked by some of the Aunts to help train their daughters, to share the secrets of how exactly she is able to rip herself in half, to break apart and dissolve. Even so, Mem's last job the week the article comes out is a relief. She has been working one site after another, filing past the rows of tombstones and the cones of plastic flowers with her handkerchief ready, speaking to no one, distracting herself by running through a list of all the words the clergy use so that they don't have to say that someone is *dead*. So far she has heard *depart, perish, sleep, expire, succumb, fall, go to a last reward, be at rest, pass, pass on,* and *pass away*, but Mem doesn't like any of these. They all seem like lies to her. The words Mem likes best are the ones used by other children, younger people who are not mourning. These are words they are not supposed to say but Mem hears them whispered anyway. *Give up the ghost. Kick the bucket. Buy the farm. Croak. Push up daisies. Check out. Stone cold. Drop dead.* Her favorite is when they call the person a *stiff*. This is an example of appropriate naming, Mem thinks, calling something exactly what it is.

It is amazing to Mem how unreliable most other words can be, amazing the things one mouth can create, surprises popping out like tricks pulled from a magician's hat. Even more amazing what a mouth can become: scissors, spikes, salve, guru, envy, comfort, chain, door. Open door. Locked door. A door with ten thousand keyholes and no keys. One keyhole and ten thousand keys that each can fit but only at very specific, very unpredictable moments.

To celebrate Mem's birthday, Mem's mother takes Mem and Sofie and Aunt Ayin to a restaurant, something they rarely do. The restaurant is decorated in a sea-ship theme. Fishing nets and life-savers are nailed to the wall and the windows are trimmed in very dark wood that has been polished to a high gloss. The paper placemats are decorated with black-and-white starfish, anchors, and lighthouses that you can color-in using a small box of crayons on the table. Mem wants to color-in her starfish while she waits for her hamburger but the crayon box only contains an unpeeled brown crayon and half of a white one that is smudged with other colors.

At the end of the meal the pretty blond waitress brings out a little cake, white with pink frosting that spells out *Happy Birthday*. Then waitress takes Mem's hand. "We have a magic treasure chest full of special treasures," she says, using her other hand to shake a large loop hung with dozens of keys. "You can try one key in the lock. If your special key works and the lock opens, you can pick out one special treasure because it's your special day!"

The trunk is plastic, a comic-book version of pirates' buried treasure. Mem takes one look at the trunk and knows that any key she uses will work. Under the bright light from above the treasure chest Mem is able to get a better look at her waitress, and now she can see all of the makeup the waitress has used to look a little younger, the small ridges around her eyes and mouth where the foundation has caked. Her eyes don't look as bright and cheery as her voice. They are snuffed out, like the dark end of an already-burned match. Washed out, as if the waitress's face has been scrubbed too hard, left too long in bleach, and then tumble-dried on the highest setting.

"Go ahead, birthday girl!" chirps the waitress. Mem tries to smile at her and make a big show of trying to pick the right key, hemming and hawing over which one it might be. And, for just a second, as she slips the key into the lock, Mem hopes that the key won't work at all, that the waitress won't have to feel like a liar today.

But it does work.

Click! goes the key in the lock. "Yay!" claps the waitress. Aunt Ayin and Mem's mother clap in the background, too. Mem's mother is smoking a cigarette, and the smoke veils her mouth so that Mem can't tell if she's smiling.

"Now go ahead and pick out one special treasure for yourself!"

The chest is full of small, depressing plastic toys. Water guns. Baby-doll bottles. Spinning tops. Little rings with water-squirting pods. Mem picks out a pen shaped like a lollipop. She looks at the waitress and says, quietly, "Thank you," and then "I'm sorry," and hands the key ring back.

When they get up to leave the restaurant and no one is looking, Mem picks her mother's smashed-down cigarette butt out of the ashtray and puts it in her pocket. The strong smell of smoke and ash clings to her fingers for hours. Later, alone in her room, Mem makes a thin hole through the filter with a sharp pencil and threads an old beaded keychain through it. She hides it in her closet, underneath a pair of Mary Janes.

That night, when Mem is supposed to be asleep, she quietly takes the keychain out of her closet and examines it. Just looking at the cigarette butt, just holding it in her hands, fills Mem with a longing she doesn't understand. She thinks this feeling is the feeling of love, the feeling of being filled up. Years later Mem will learn that it is the other way around; it is the feeling of having too many holes, deep thrumming need-holes that can never be filled. Years later Mem will find the cigarette keychain and feel the same longing, but she will be better prepared for it then, she will understand everything there is to know about holes. She will know it is a waste of time to try to fill them.

For now, she looks at the keychain and loves her mother so much she doesn't know what to do with all the love. But loving Mem's mother means hopping from stone to stone, trying to cross treacherous and shark-infested waters. Mem never knows when she might lose her balance, or slip, or be too afraid to keep going. The words from her mother's mouth stick to Mem and absorb into her skin. They get trapped between her teeth. They itch the soles of her feet. They lie in wait, preparing to be hatched.

The next morning Mem's mother decides that Mem and Sofie should stay with one of the Aunts for a while, perhaps a week or two, until the attention from the article dies down. Mem's mother decides to take advantage of the girls' week or two away to do a little business in Connecticut. "Fuck that politician, DePaul," she says. "It's times like this I wish I could vote."

While her mother packs, Mem sulks, following her mother from room to room. "But *why* can't I go with you?" she asks.

Her mother doesn't look up from what she is doing. "Don't whine," she says. "Nobody likes a whiner."

"Well why can't I?" asks Mem, then, using a more grown-up voice. "I could help."

"There's nothing for you to do," says her mother. She stops what she's doing and looks at Mem. "Besides, if I take you, Ayin will insist on taking Sofie with and we can't afford the four of us going. God knows how I'm going to afford feeding just Ayin. You're safer here. And you're going to love Aunt Raziel." Mem isn't sure how she is going to love someone she's never even met. Although anything is better than staying with Aunt Ayin, who reads stories about poisons and antidotes and cooks slimy brussel sprouts that taste like farts and then fawns over Sofie's drawings and says that Mem's "could be better."

When Aunt Ayin drops Mem and Sofie off at Aunt Raziel's apartment, in a towering complex in the northeast part of the city, Mem notices that all of the shopping centers around the complex are flanked by lumpy, diseased trees and strangely lettered signs that Mem can't understand.

"That's Russian," Aunt Ayin explains. "A lot of Russians live here now."

"Is Aunt Raziel Russian?" asks Sofie.

"No," says Aunt Ayin. "She's from Poland. She survived the Holocaust."

Mem's mother has explained to her, a few times, how millions of people were gassed to death because they were Jewish. Mem didn't realize before that there were people who had survived. *There have been holocausts like that all over the world for all different kinds of people since the beginning of time,* Mem's mother had said. *There are even some holocausts happening now. But the Nazi Holocaust was run like a factory. They put millions of people in ovens.* Aunt Raziel must be bitter, Mem thinks, and tough as nails. *Raziel, angel of the sublime secrets and supreme mysteries.* Wise, but bitter, like cooked chicken hearts.

They ride the elevator up to the seventh floor. The hallway carpet is black, with neon-colored geometrical shapes and dots on top. In front of each apartment door the shapes and colors look dirty and smushed down. Florescent lights flicker on the ceiling like long and irritated blinking eyes.

"Here we are," says Aunt Ayin, stopping to knock on one of the doors.

Mem and Sofie glance nervously at each other. On the way over, Aunt Ayin told them that Aunt Raziel sports heart-shaped eyeglasses which she has specially made, that her thin hair is dyed jet black, and that she wears pink lipstick and will dance, alone, to any kind of music that happens to be playing, even if she is just having lunch in somebody's house, even if people stare at her and point. Aunt Raziel is a fortune teller who gave up wailing long ago but is still considered an honorary Master Wailer. She has a deep accent and can speak six different languages.

"And," Aunt Ayin added with a flourish, "Raziel looks like a real gypsy."

Mem stares up at the peephole, wondering who is on the other side, when the door is opened by a small, shawl-covered lady wearing bright purple lipstick and red high heels, smiling and calling out, "Well, my pretty little ladies, don't just stand there! Come in! Come in!"

After some fuss once Aunt Ayin says she must go, and thank you so much, and hope they won't be any bother, Mem and Sofie are steered inside the apartment. Mem sees a crystal ball, a set of tarot cards laid out on top of a picnic table, three old, sleepy dogs, and a tiny balcony overlooking the back of a Russian kosher fish store. There is also a big television set, which makes Mem catch her breath. The girls have heard about television but have never been allowed to see one before.

Aunt Raziel tells them to put their bags down and relax on the love seat, a threadbare couch covered in several layers of dog hair. Mem and Sofie sit down, slowly, their eyes darting around the room. The crystal ball seems to be the only clean thing in the apartment.

Aunt Raziel settles herself into a folding chair and smiles. Her teeth are yellow, some of them cracked. "Are you hungry?" she asks. They both shake their heads no. "You like the crystal ball, yes?" she asks. They nod their heads yes. "Don't you talk?" she asks, and starts to laugh. Mem and Sofie laugh, too.

"Why haven't we ever seen you at any jobs?" asks Mem. "Did your eyes dry up?"

Aunt Raziel lights what looks like a thin brown cigarette (it's actually a miniature cigar, she tells them later, a *cigarillo*) and the room is infused with a sweet blue smoke. She shrugs. "I had to mourn for a long time," she says. "I don't want to mourn anymore."

How wonderful, Mem thinks, to just decide that you're done, that you don't want to do it anymore. How wonderful to be allowed to stop.

"Now I tell fortunes instead," says Aunt Raziel, the skin around her almond-shaped eyes crinkling as she smiles. "People in this country pays a lot of money to find out what happens in their past lives, or what happen in the future. Even though they can't change none of it."

She purses her lips around the cigarillo and explains that her special powers came to her when she was a little girl starving in Belsen. Looking up at a watchtower one day she saw the ghost of her dead brother standing where an SS soldier should have been and took this as a sign that the end was near. She was right; a few days later, the Allies liberated her camp. By some miracle, Aunt Raziel and both her parents survived, although six months later, her parents were stabbed to death during a pogrom in Poland. Aunt Raziel was stabbed in the chest four times, and lived.

Although Aunt Raziel is named for the angel of the secret regions, she doesn't seem to have any secrets anymore. Whatever secrets she might have had were burned out of her, tortured out of her with sticks and knives and guns. Starved out of her like tapeworms. Her true story is so severe that it has left nothing but the truth. And psychic powers that she uses to see into people's past lives.

"One of my cousins was in the death march," she says. "Almost all the other girls died but she survives. You know why?"

Mem and Sofie shake their heads.

"She was wearing her winter boots when they first take her away, big black boots, even though it is summertime. Somehow, she knows she should be wearing those boots. During the march in the snow, my cousin is the one who keeps walking. She was fifteen years old. When the Americans finds her she weighs sixty pounds."

Mem doesn't know what to say to this. A *death march*: a march to your own death, or someone else's? She remembers her big snowboots, black with heavy tread and a dozen hooks for the laces.

"Do you want me to read your cards?" Aunt Raziel asks Mem.

Mem looks at the cards on the coffee table, their frighteningly expressionless cartoon faces, and says, "No thank you." Sofie shakes her head no, too.

The living room is thick with flies and the earthy stench of Aunt Raziel's three old dogs. In the apartment above Aunt Raziel someone clomps angrily from room to room. The only food in the kitchen is a collection of complimentary bits Aunt Raziel has stolen from restaurants, airports, and offices—tiny parcels of sugar, salt and pepper, small breadsticks in cellophane, instant coffee and little creamers, packets of half-crushed crackers. But, surveying all of the detritus, Mem knows, by instinct, that she is protected. She will never have a nightmare here.

— 1988 A.D., PENNSYLVANIA, U.S.A. —

LETTER FRAGMENT
Author Unknown

August 28, 1988

I know you will understand why I must do it. I have begun to find the time between funerals unbearable, and watching her from a distance has simply become no longer enough. While her mother's profitable features include an obvious health and voluminous sexual appeal, it is the girl's lack of physical endowment which creates such a contrary effect and triggers within me a desire, an urgency, unlike any I have known before. It is worth noting that the mother's public performances often call to mind the great pomp of British seventeenth-century funeral traditions and are typically quite commanding; her control is commendable and she has, on many occasions, attempted to use her obvious erotic charisma to sway my attention from our negotiations, distracting me with steady, subtle directives to her eyes, mouth, breasts, and hands. Unlike the girl, who seems to sustain as little body as necessary to exist in a three-dimensional world, the mother can easily slip into a realm where she is all body and, therefore, all temptation, without ever openly offering anything at all. Being involved only so much as to gain valuable sociological insights, I myself have never responded to the elusive suggestions presented by the girl's mother, but I have witnessed its potently reductive power over men and women alike at gravesites; this perhaps reveals to us the vigorous connection between the oppositional events of procreation and death. The girl's performances, however, are compelling for precisely the opposite reason. She seems at times so bodiless and bloodless, translucent as vellum, then sometimes shadowy, hardly sustaining flesh and form; she does not entice with the body but the thing within the body which is howling to escape; the girl does not appear conscious of this at all, she seems to see herself as temporary. She is always just barely there.

9

"Have you ever lived in hiding?"

Every morning, no matter what the weather, Aunt Raziel prepares a cup of stolen instant coffee, drags her mother's ratty mouton coat over her nightgown, lights a cigarillo, and stands on her dilapidated balcony, smoking and sipping coffee and feeling the sun on her face. When she comes back in she opens two little plastic creamers and adds a few drops of coffee to each one, one for Mem and one for Sofie. They sit on her dog-hair-covered couch in their pajamas and dip breadsticks and giggle while Aunt Raziel tells them about their past lives.

Mem, she says, has an old soul, which gives her an innate sense of right and wrong. Mem was often a man and once drowned while swimming frantically to a ship. She was a happy little girl playing by the side of a lake. She was once in a war, which was why she always jumps whenever she hears a loud noise. Mem wants to believe these things. She feels in her bones that they are true. She imagines herself in the body of a large man, gasping for air as the waves slap against her face, forcing lungfuls of saltwater into her mouth.

Aunt Raziel says that she, herself, has left her body many times. She sees accidents happening countries away. When she touches a pregnant woman, she can feel the flicker of life moving inside her own womb. Mem listens, petting one of the wretched old dogs, the blind, shaggy brown one who seems to like her. Aunt Raziel is convinced that dogs are noble creatures and that her hound has taken a liking to Mem because she is special. Mem wants her to think this. She strokes the dog's nappy fur and looks soulfully into his eyes and asks Aunt Raziel what she can do to make sure that she doesn't have to come back ever again.

Aunt Raziel looks slightly stricken. "You don't want to come back to Aunt Raziel's apartment?" she asks.

"Oh, no, I'm sorry," Mem says, quickly. "I mean, I don't want to come back, anywhere, after I die."

Aunt Raziel looks deep into Mem's eyes. Her own eyes are long. Sad. Crinkle-edged. She tells Mem that few people live such fulfilled lives that they never return. But there are some things Mem could do, she adds, things that could help: Be honest. Do good deeds for others. Use all talents as often as possible. Never be lazy.

Mem's heart sinks.

Lazyfilthyliar.

She is trapped.

She will have to come back and do this all over again, forever and ever, because she will never be able to get it right. *A million keys, none of them right.* What if Mem is so bad in this life that she's sent back as a cockroach, or a flea? Is the life of a flea equal to the life of a person? How many fleas does it take to equal a person? Who makes these decisions?

"Don't think about it too much, sweetheart," says Aunt Raziel. "We all have the body of animals and the souls of angels."

After finishing their coffees, Mem and Sofie each take a bath in Aunt Raziel's peach-colored bathroom, spraying themselves luxuriously with a hand-held shower head. They rummage through Raziel's old junk drawers and discover powder puffs on wands, ancient lipsticks that smell like crayons, and silver tiaras with some of the rhinestones missing. They put all of these things on and run outside onto the balcony, even though Aunt Raziel warns them that their still-wet hair might freeze.

Aunt Raziel's bathroom is small and crammed with dozens of tiny perfume bottles. The bottles are delicate and dust-laden and full of liquids the same color as the brandy Aunt Raziel keeps in the kitchen in a crystal decanter. Next to the toilet is a wicker wastebasket full of old *Reader's Digests*, water-warped covers yelling article titles like "Trapped!" or "How I Survived." Mem loves these magazines. Every story features good people and bad people. In the end, the bad people get what they deserve and the good people are rescued. Even the sad stories have happy endings, like *Trapped!*, a story about a family on vacation that suffered severe frostbite when an avalanche covered their cabin. While Aunt Raziel walks the dogs or goes shopping or reads cards for clients over the phone, Mem and Sofie page through the *Reader's Digests*, or lounge on the couch in their borrowed finery, watching the television for hours on end.

They have never seen anything like it and are reluctant to leave the television, even to pee, even during commercials. It's like a window into the world of the unprofessionals.

There are talk shows with people who are dressed up but damaged, like shiny but bruised apples. *My father used to electrocute me*, cries the four-hundred-pound woman who can barely fit on the two chairs the show has set out for her. Next to her, on the table, the box of tissues has its own spotlight.

There seem to be awful things happening to women all over the world. Cut tongues, ribs removed, girl babies suffocated at birth. Mem watches flickers of people with exotic colors for skin walking toward borders, area rugs wrapped around their shoulders. Some of these had other people put their children and grandmothers on trucks going toward the border and now cannot find them. Then a woman with a bicycle helmet of hair reads the daily horoscope. Through shellacked mauve lips the woman says, *Aquarius. Listen to your inner self. Make and return calls. Tonight, be happy at home.*

Mem struggles with this word, *self*, which is used a good deal by people on the television. *Tell me about your self.* She knows what it means but is not sure of what it means for her, although she thinks she knows who she *is*. She is her mother's daughter, a Wailer, a pretty child, someone who loves, a star, a lady, a talented girl. But she is also an embarrassment, a disgusting soul, a waste of flesh, short and strange and somewhat grotesque, stupid, sorry, sad, a person whose life is not quite worth the air she breathes or the physical space she takes. Is all of this her self? Does all of this manage to coexist, shifting, scrambling and separating, inside of her? Maybe none of these are true. Maybe beneath the fitful clash of these discordant ideas exists an unimaginable void where her self is supposed to be.

Mem feels gratified when, late in the evenings, she sees reviews for films called *tearjerkers*, where actors make money by pretending to cry. Then there are shows about near-death experiences (*fools*, says Aunt Raziel from the balcony, *all of life is a near-death experience*), science shows, painting shows, cooking shows. People on television seem to cry for any old reason, not just for the dead. They even cry when they're happy, or relieved. Mem is shocked to discover how much the followers of Christ value tears, how their TV preachers are able to cry and stop crying like Wailers.

But Mem doesn't understand the way that death is portrayed on television. Soap opera widows fall in love with someone new after just a few days of grieving. On action shows, the *bad guy* kills one person while the *good guy* kills thirty just to find the bad guy. Mem is surprised—and saddened—that they hardly ever show the funerals for these dead people. And why, she wonders, don't cartoon characters really die? They get steamrollered and dropped from caldrons and smashed by anvils and squashed into accordion shapes but are always able to pop up or puff themselves back to their original shapes. Then there are the old black-and-white movies about zombies and vampires and monsters, all of whom supposedly rise from the dead. Sofie can barely watch these movies, but none of them frighten Mem, who has seen the deceased close up and knows that there is no rising from the dead, that these zombies wouldn't be able to see because their eyes would have rotted out years ago.

While watching the television, Mem and Sofie learn that there are other girls, in equally questionable professions, who are double-named, too—whores, dancers, circus freaks, gypsies, and superheroes. These characters have distinct double-names that don't seem to be attached to each other. They are each attached, instead, to very different identities. If the whore on the street (wearing scratched thigh-high boots held up by rubber bands with legs lumping out like rum-raisin ice cream packed into two pink pleather cones) is named *Candy*, there is a complete someone-else underneath, waiting to come up with the sun, maybe someone named *Sarah* (who wears sensible shoes and reading glasses while she studies in the library). For girls like these, the double-names switch and shift and have different hues to them. It seems they can change their identities as easily as taking off one outfit called *Candy* and putting on another called *Sarah*. Even the superheroes, who look pretty much the same in or out of costume, can make this transformation by just taking off a suit jacket or letting down their hair.

But once Mem has time to think about it, seriously sipping her cream-er-with-coffee, she begins to see it differently. Maybe the real identity of these double-named girls, she thinks, the secret identity, is actually under-neath both of the names, like a fan dancer hidden beneath her two moving fans. With grace and deft maneuvering, the double-named girl can conceal her secret self behind one name, then the other, without ever revealing what was underneath. *Candy* (flap, rustle, whoosh)...*Sarah* (whisk, swoosh) ...*Candy* (flicker, flash, sweep)...

Mem's double-naming, however, is not graceful. Her names don't stroke across her like elegant white plumes. Her double-naming is, instead, a pair of Siamese twins stuck at the chest and sharing the same heart, dou-ble mouths moving no matter which one is speaking. The two names *Mem* and *Mirabelle* hum out at the lips all at once. They dissolve into one anoth-er like salt and water that can never be boiled apart. Mem and Mirabelle share the same old black dooles. The same old black shoes. The same hair. Neither wears glasses.

Mem knows that if she had to do a fan dance she would never be able to manage two sumptuous, Mem-sized sprays of quills. She would be clumsy. She would drop one fan and, concealing herself behind the other fan, bend over to retrieve the first fan and drop the second one in its place. The hollow spines of the fan would clatter against the wooden stage and snap off under her toes. Loose fan fibers would float, making Mem sneeze.

She would sweat. The fans would be too heavy to keep lifting. The men in the audience would start to stir. *Is this what we paid for?* they'd call out. *I want my money back.* Smiling nervously, Mem would try to whisk the fans in front of one another but her arms would be too small, the fans would only jerk into each other like cymbals, over and over again until they knocked themselves right out of her hands, falling in a heap like giant, just-shot geese.

Then Mem would be naked on the stage, trying to hide her feet under her fans, and someone would cry out *Look at yourself! Look at yourself!*

And, peering downward, Mem would look at herself.

And all the men would laugh and point.

But this is not how Aunt Raziel sees her. She tells Mem, "You are gorgeous, Mem, you are gifted. You are a special girl, I see this." When the visit is over and it's time for the girls to go home, the goodbye is teary. Mem cannot bear to leave Raziel, the balcony, the dogs and all of their fur. But by the time Aunt Ayin drops Mem off at home, Mem is almost giddy, unable to wait to tell her mother about all of the things she has seen. She swings the storm door open and bounds into the foyer. The storm door's pneumatic hinge closes behind her with its familiar hiss, but beneath it is another sound, the sound of someone else in the house.

Mem can tell by the voice that it's a man. Mem drops her sack and stands behind the foyer doorway, peeking out into the dining room from behind the woodwork, and sees that it is an old man, obediently stooped, hat in hand, nodding at whatever Mem's mother has just said.

"Thank you so much for making this appointment so quickly," he says, running the damp rim of his hat through his hands. "When I saw the article I knew I had to contact you."

And then Mem sees them: a salt-and-pepper mustache under big, crusty nostrils, meaty fingers like sausages wrapped in dry leaves.

"I'm sorry, I look such a mess," he adds apologetically, laughing a little, brushing the white cat hairs from the lap of his coffee-colored tweed. "I have three cats, you know." Waves of scalp-smell waft over to where Mem is standing. Oily, warm, sweetish.

The man sees Mem standing behind the woodwork and squints his watery eyes. "Ah!" he says, grinning. "The lady of the hour."

"Would you care for something to drink?" asks Mem's mother, leading him further into the house, deeper into the place where Mem lives. She pulls out a living room chair and motions for him to sit down. Mem doesn't move from behind the woodwork. She holds onto the doorframe and watches.

"No, nothing for me, thank you," says the man, waving his hat a little. It takes him a while to sit down. Mem's mother finds Mem clinging to the woodwork and gets down onto one knee. She touches Mem's elbows. She is so beautiful to look at that Mem has to hold her breath.

"Listen, baby," she whispers. "This man has come a long way and is willing to pay a lot of money for you to wail for him. He just wants a few minutes. I've seen you do ten minutes without even trying."

Mem shakes her head. Her mother clucks her tongue and smiles.

"Come on, sweetheart. Go put on your blacks. It'll be easy."

"But I don't feel sad now," Mem answers.

Mem's mother stands up, laughing, and grabs Mem's hand.

"Don't be silly," she says.

— 1988 A.D., PENNSYLVANIA, U.S.A. —

LETTER FRAGMENT
Author Unknown

September 15, 1988

I am certain and thus saddened that the girl's astounding genius is being squandered upon a vulgar and ignorant audience, a true case of pearls before swine if ever there was one, so it is understandable why I am so thrilled to announce that, after much negotiation with her mother, I have finally been granted private (and therefore exorbitantly expensive) audience with "Mirabelle." As per my specific requests, she is to wail for me in her own home; I am confident that conducting our meeting in the "wailer's" concealed domain will allow the girl to feel more comfortable revealing something to me that would otherwise be out of the question. As an "unprofessional," I am aware of my lowly rank and powerlessness in Mirabelle's eyes, but if I can get her to see herself as I see her—a gifted, complex, and lovely child—perhaps she will begin to cultivate a sense of safety with my presence. I must admit (though with great reticence), were it not for the remarkably detailed (though not particularly well-written) articles featuring the enchanting and elusive "Mirabelle," this already trying pursuit would have been soon rendered hopeless, little more than the quixotic fancy of a silly old man. I am hopeful that my upcoming appointment will oblige the mother to withdraw the girl from the illegal and limiting world of burial mourning and begin, instead, to take up a regular private practice. My fear is that by becoming entertainment for the masses—and because of the exposing nature of her work—the girl may someday suffer a great indignity for her public (I have oft wondered if it is at all possible to achieve fame without first enduring indignity; perhaps it is not possible to exhibit one's self without leaving some part of that self behind?). To those of us lucky enough to have witnessed the performances, it is clear that the crying of this frail ingénue is not a dramatic indulgence; it is, in fact, her total lack of technique and palpable reticence which makes her work so gripping; I have, of course, considered the possibility that the girl's reticence might be calculated, an ancestral method well-rehearsed so as to heighten the emotional experience of the client (as well as the fee for her work), but I am willing to temporarily suspend all skepticism until the sotto voce performance is complete.

10

"Do you ever perform for clients in private?"

The door is closing in the playroom, where Mem and the man sit around the old card table. The tweed on the old man's jacket is cloudy with cat hair. Mem stares at the jacket and uses her fingernails to pick at the edges of the sticky strips of shelf-paper glued to the table.

The door closes and the man puts his meaty fingers on her knee. The moment his fingers touch her she can't move.

"Stand up for me," he says, gently. "Stand up in front of the mirror."

Mem does what he says, getting up and moving in front of the tall mirror that leans against the wall. There she is, yes, it is her in the reflection, wearing her blacks, looking much smaller than she feels. Looking scared. "Don't be scared," he says and he stands up, too.

He stands behind her, clamping his hands onto her shoulders. "Start crying," he whispers into her hair. "If you don't do it, I will have to call the police and turn your mother in, and then you will never see her again. I wouldn't want something like that to happen, would you? Start crying."

She starts crying. It isn't hard to cry but it is hard to watch herself crying in the big beveled mirror with pretty cherries and cherubs carved into the frame. Her reflection looks strange, shrinking. The man nods and smiles. His hands fumble forward a little, touching Mem's nipples over her doole.

She is watching it happen, in the mirror. He watches her watching his fingers. Then he closes his eyes, pressing himself against her bottom, rubbing. He opens his eyes. Rubbing. He says, breathlessly, throaty, "Look at yourself in the mirror. You are so lovely! You don't even know how lovely you are. Look at yourself. Aren't you lovely?"

Mem's skin feels feverish, like when she's sick and her mother sprinkles the bed with talcum powder and feeds her toast-and-jelly soaked in tea. Like when her skin hurts so bad she's afraid to move, afraid that if she turns over, the wrinkles in her sheets will leave bruises.

"Keep crying."

She watches the mirror, watches the man watching her.

What does she say? Does she whisper? Does she shriek? Mem can just make it out, the movement of her lips, the sound of the man's voice coming out from between them, saying *don't tell, don't tell...so lovely...*

That night, for supper, Mem's mother makes homemade M-shaped pancakes. Puffy, syrup-soaked Ms that Mem doesn't want to eat. She chews their spongy sweetness and her stomach fills with the feeling she gets when they drive on the serpentine roller-coaster road, only the feeling isn't going up and down like the humps on the street. Instead it just stays there, semi-solid, its insides whirling while Mem chews and chews and chews.

The man left a ghost of himself there, too, lingering in the house like an old smell. Mem can't see the ghost but she can feel him. He is watching her. He is right behind her. He is everywhere. He is inside her.

Mem dutifully swallows the Ms on her plate. Her mother hums softly to herself while she tidies up. Her humming is made of Ms, too. *M* for *Mr. M with a Mustached Mouth. M* for *Mirror. M* for *Monster.*

And *M* for *Money,* which Mem's mother counts out onto the kitchen table, each hundred-dollar bill at a time.

— 1629 A.D., WESTPHALIA, PRUSSIA —
EXCERPTS FROM A LETTER TO THE CITY COMMISSIONER

As to your query concerning the fate of those persecuted: Like you, we, too, believed the weeping maids affair was finished, but it has resurfaced in a fashion beyond description…two weeks ago a maid of twelve was hanged, of whom it was said she was the most virtuous, most unspoiled in the city…accused of weeping for payment, engaging in coitus with demons, rendering men impotent, and poisoning her hands with ointment while acting as midwife before delivery…There are still dozens in the city involved, of all ages, and of high and low fortune, and even pious, so vehemently condemned that they may be seized at any moment. It is beyond doubt that a great many of the King's people, of all classes and offices, must be [put to death], including scholarly members of the Court, and its medical practitioners, and those who serve the county, many with whom you are mostly well acquainted;……I am not able to describe any more of this agony. Know that there will be yet more esteemed persons with whom you are familiar and of whom you think highly…Fiat justitia…no rank is spared, no man, woman or child above suspicion. I implore you: it is dangerous to attempt to save those accused, do not try.

11

"Do you believe in ghosts?"

Mem and Sofie are playing Funeral in the spare bedroom when they hear Mem's mother calling. *Girls, girls, come down.* The girls reach the top landing and try to walk down the stairs and they see that the steps are covered in guts, slippery pink entrails that move as if breathing. *It's okay,* Mem says, and she takes Sofie's hand. Barefooted, they step carefully, but a few pieces of guts squish between Mem's toes. Downstairs, Aunt Ayin and Mem's mother are eating supper at the dining room table, their forks lightly scraping against the good china. The light in the dining room is harsh and makes sullen shadows under the grown-ups' eyes and noses. *How old are you?* Ayin asks Mem, and when Mem says, *I'm almost eleven* she can hardly hear her own voice.

Girls, girls, come here, says Mem's mother. She catches hold of Mem's other hand and squeezes it as Mem looks out the dining room window and sees, pale in the black darkness, her mother walking by, looking right at her. How can this be? She can feel her mother's cool hand in her own but the woman on the other side of the window is clearly also her mother. Panicked, Mem looks at Sofie, who smiles, and Mem knows it is too late.

Mem tries to pry her fingers away from Sofie but it is impossible, Sofie is already strong with ghost force, her fixed smile gleaming, glimmering dog's teeth, and the pounding sound of footsteps rushes into the room and Mem knows it isn't Sofie anymore, it is the someone-else, the ghost, and it is starting to hurt her, pushing its fingers onto Mem's body, trying to tickle her but it doesn't tickle, it hurts so bad it is like dying.

The pictures on the wall are of people Mem doesn't know, looking away, at something else. Mem wraps her hands around the not-Sofie's wrists and tries to get it off but the not-Sofie doesn't budge. Mem twists and turns and tries to get away. The fingers are tentacles and huge. Mem fights them off, angry at herself; she should have grabbed the not-Sofie's fingers, not its wrists, because now its fingers can grow and get at her, no matter how much she struggles.

The not-Sofie keeps smiling. The feeling in Mem's stomach where the fingers press is too much, worse than nausea, it make Mem want to crawl out of her skin. Does she hear her mother say *look at yourself such a pretty girl aren't you lovely?* Mem can't hear well, the pounding is so loud, like footsteps approaching on the floor above, like someone is walking right through her. The pain is coming out of Mem's mouth. The pain is bigger than Mem.

Mem cries and begs, *No, please, not again* and her mother is finally there in the room again, but she isn't watching. She is looking away, out the window, at something else.

When Mem wakes up she remembers, *I am the legend, I am beloved*, but she feels disoriented, confused, for a second not knowing where she is, not recognizing any of the objects in her room. Her heart pounds with the rhythm of the phantom footsteps. The ghosts could be anywhere now, having escaped from the dream. Mem tries to calm herself. She tells herself there are good ghosts and bad ghosts and someday the bad ghosts will go away. But Mem doesn't really believe that the bad dreams will ever really go away. They have been waiting for her at the end of each day for months now, predators under the sheets, angry and gray. The color gray is for ghosts who came after Mem in her sleep, gray for the thumping sound they make as they walk through her dreams in an angry parade. Gray for how hard it is to see them. In her dreams Mem can be anywhere but the ghosts are always there, hiding. Mem never knows when they might come because they can disguise themselves as people she knows, people she loves. Once they came looking like the neighbor's dog. Once it was Aunt Ayin. A million times it is her mother.

In Mem's waking life, her mother is mostly proud and loving, especially now that Mem is one of the only Wailers people will still hire. Things have changed. Now there are two cremations for every five deaths, and Mem's fantastic notions of bone-choked green spaces are replaced with images of sandy ash piles clogging rivers, ashes in the food, ashes in the air so that everyone will soon be forced to breathe their dead. But Mem is so well-respected that she is hired to wail for these scattered cremains— both the disposals and the pick-up-and-burns. Mem has become so marketable, is in such high demand, that she is hired to weep for whole families as they die off in clusters, as older loved ones tend to do. She is hired to wail for dead children. She is even hired to wail for the very rich men who die, usually an impossible population to penetrate because their very young and well-coifed wives don't usually like to be outmourned.

But Mem's mother does not want Mem, who will soon be a teenager and thus not as young-looking, to take her fame for granted. She tells Mem that the mighty and prosperous Aurora, once endowed with a Master's talent and an eternity in which to perform it, soon became Aurora, little-known goddess, burdened with a most important and painful task, her immortality a strain, then transformed into Aurora, completely forgotten Roman goddess, barely even indexed in reference books about antiquity. And now, Aurora, the name of a distant galaxy. A ruin.

Once, while Mem was looking at her mother's framed photographs of Rome and the *Via Salaria*, she asked Aunt Ayin about the random ruins exposed right in the middle of modern city blocks. Aunt Ayin said that because there were so many ruins in Rome, there were ghosts everywhere and that the residents of Rome accept them as part of their lives, like stray cats.

"Bullshit," said Mem's mother, rushing past them to scoop the *schmutz* off the top of the boiling chicken soup. "Don't feed the girl lies, Ayin. You've never even been to Rome."

After huffing and harrumphing and adjusting her too-tight doole, Aunt Ayin told Mem that the zephyrs winding through the small streets of Rome bounce off the cobblestones like lost change and in them you can hear the small voices of dead children ringing. There are footprints everywhere that can not be accounted for. Small voices rustling through linens in the closets. Messages written in the dust. The ghosts of Rome are like house-guests that wouldn't go away, she said, opening her round eyes wide. The residents learn to live with them and their anxious petulance, taking them for granted until the best plums go missing or shoes disappear. Desperate gamblers take poor advice from utterings that they mistake for intuition. At night the dogs growl at nothing. The children talk to themselves.

Mem had nodded, solemn, pursing her lips together. She could tell from Aunt Ayin's distilled expression that she had never actually seen a ghost herself.

Lucky you, thought Mem.

Ever since the old man has been inside her house, the ghost part of Mem's self has solidified; it is dense and rigid as pewter now, silvery, non-porous, cold. But Mem knows that there are ghosts, other ghosts, living in her house. She has suspected this since she was younger, but now she feels it, deep down inside her. There is always a silent audience, like the photo of her grandmother over the mantel. Watching, judging, taking notes. She can feel them but she can't see them, they are invisible and as adhesive as the pieces of gauze that stick to you when you accidentally walk through a cobweb. Mem knows she is never alone in her house.

Even though the outside of Mem's house isn't scary at all, it is the inside that Mem finds frightening, especially at night. The basement stairwell, the clean corners, the creaking gray bubbles of air under the confetti-colored carpets. Mem has seen other houses, older, more expensive single homes with sleeping monster eyes for windows, screaming mouths for doors. Horrifying houses of shut-up faces, flat eyes hideously separated and shrouded with screens. Whenever Mem looks at her house through the back window of her mother's car she thinks the front of her house doesn't look anything like a face. The windows are too modern, too set into the deep siding to look like eyes. The blue door is off-center, not at all mouth-like. But sometimes it feels like there is another house inside Mem's house, hidden and hard to see, with other doors and rooms Mem doesn't know about. A dark gray house she only visits in her dreams.

In bed at night, Mem stares at the blue-black air and feels she is lost somewhere inside of it, that she cannot find herself. She watches the air around her burn slowly from blue to maroon, angry lava rusting in its shell of black. By early morning the air is red, having slowly grown blood-colored bark. Rust red. Snake red. And black-and-blue bruise black, *lazyfilthyliaruglysmellyweird* black but edged in a thick crimson hide. The sodden gray of shadows, of half-memories undulating their limbs under water. The grays of ghosts thumping through Mem's bed in their angry parade, dragging their heavy-footed vapor down the hallway to her room.

A few days before her eleventh birthday, Mem is hired to weep at a funeral for a man who threw himself out of a window. The deceased's name is Edgar, he was seventy-five years old, a retired tool-and-die maker who had been married for fifty years. There were no children. There was no suicide note. In the newspaper clipping that Edgar's wife sends, Mem reads that Edgar jumped from the 22nd floor of their apartment building the week before, crashing head-first on the sidewalk at about 3:30 p.m. He died instantly, landing next to a pedestrian who had to be treated at a nearby hospital for trauma. Dozens of business people, tourists, and street vendors flocked around Edgar's body, which police had to cover up with a bedsheet. Some of the people, probably the tourists, tried to take photographs of the scene, so police held up more sheets to impede their view.

Edgar's widow calls to request that Mem come to her South Philly apartment to go over all the details. She explains that she once saw Mem work another funeral and was very impressed. Having no children of her own, she feels the need to hire a younger mourner, someone who will grieve for Edgar, she says, "Like a daughter would, if we'd had one."

Mem gladly accepts the job because she has been thinking a great deal about this kind of thing, which way she would like to die, and has decided that falling would be the best way to go. There must have been a moment for Edgar when the falling became flying. Or perhaps it's the other way around: you fly for a while until you realize you are just falling. Aunt Ayin says that if you fall in a dream and actually hit bottom you will never wake up again. Mem has dreams where she's falling, from cliffs or rooftops or the tips of mountains, and she always hits the ground, hard—so hard that once the shock subsides and Mem gets up from falling, she sees a body-shaped imprint in the soil and feels a twisting drop in her gut that lingers long after impact. But Mem knows that in real life, falling and flying are opposites. Edgar must have known it, too.

When Mem's mother reads the clipping about Edgar, she *tsk*s and shakes her head. Her roots are covered in blue-black wet. "Death by falling," she says, disapproving, the slow trickles of dye dripping around her ears. "It's a weakling's way to die. You make a mess."

And Edgar did make a mess. When he hit the ground his body did not leave a body-shaped smash in the cement, clear as the outlines of a cookie cutter. The cement stayed hard and smashed Edgar instead. In the bloody show-and-tell following his death, the sheets the policeman had been holding up brushed against the bone-shard stew that Edgar had become and then the sheets were not worth saving, but his wife saved them anyway, carefully washing and folding and putting them away. They were Egyptian cotton, two-hundred thread count, eggshell white with a corn-flower blue trim at the top of the flat sheet.

Edgar's wife explains all of these things to Mem as they sit in Edgar's dark living room, listening to the pendulum of the grandfather clock swish back and forth. The oscillating fan shakes its head in a slow no, spreading the same trapped breeze across the room, warm and stale as someone-else's used breath. It flutters and then drops the stray curlicues of hair around Mem's face, tickling and itching the skin of her neck.

Edgar's bloodstains came out easily with white bathroom soap and cold water, his wife explains. She is short and plump, with cropped brown hair, and wears orthopedic oxfords and a smock patterned with upside-down fir trees. She recalls how carefully she scrubbed each blood-spot over the cracked pedestal sink in the bathroom, this last bit of housework for Edgar, who, she notes, never much cared for white linens.

"The sheets are in the antique linen cupboard now," she says to Mem, adding that they had bought the cupboard on their third anniversary at a yard sale on the way to a dinner with friends Edgar had never much cared for. The sheets will probably stay there for a long time. She says she can't use them, though the bits of Edgar that used to be there are just watery shadows now, barely visible cloud-shaped stains.

She walks over to the cupboard, which has been painted over so many times that its top layer of sage green is blistered and bubbled, revealing small fractures of past colors. The uneven floorboards creak under her sturdy shoes. She opens the glass cupboard doors and there are three crisp stacks of perfectly folded white bedclothes inside.

"Some of these sets are older than you," she says to Mem. She runs her dry hands over the sheets on the top of the pile without really looking at them, the little dry peaks of skin on her palms catching like a cat's tongue on the two hundred threads of Egyptian cotton, the trim she had thought might actually go well with the bedroom curtains.

She shakes her head. She says, as if to herself, "I don't know," and walks into the kitchen to make tea. Mem watches her walk away, listening to the sound of the floor.

Edgar's wife may not know, but Mem does. She isn't going to tell this lady what she knows. She isn't going to say, *It is just easier, to not have to live. When you're dead, it all just goes away.* Who knows what secrets Edgar had been carrying around with him over the past seven decades. When you're dead, you don't have to worry about secrets anymore. When you're dead, there's nothing left that you have to protect.

On the wall next to the kitchen there is a small wooden cross hanging from an old-fashioned cut nail. Mem is beginning to find all of these symbols stupid, so much superstition everywhere, in every home, at every grave, rituals and signs and incantations carried out ceremoniously, magic spells to save the dead. Although even Mem's mother sometimes indulges in reading signs when she sees them, she always tells Mem that it was superstition that killed her grandmother. Not Ayin's absurd praying or Mem's mother's own secret wishes for laughter and pink dresses, but an old-fashioned suspension: a whole pig's heart that had been stuck with white thorns and put in the chimney for luck. It was the heart, the grand-mother's homemade charm, that had caught fire, smoldering once the family went to bed, then falling and bouncing onto the not-at-all-fireproof living room floor. A heart stuck with thorns! Like something from a witch's cupboard. Like something out of a fairytale, the old kind from Italy complete with enchanted beasts, hidden castles full of food, and gowns so fine they could be stored in small chestnuts and then pulled through the eye of a needle.

There is a tarnished silver tea service on a little shelf under the cross, a set that Edgar's wife probably never uses. Mem can see part of the reflec-tion of her face in the belly of the dull silver sugar bowl. Lately for Mem the color silver has been a secret rolling around inside of her like an anx-ious bead of mercury. The secret shines so bright she thinks it can be seen through the cracks of who she is. The secret is silver like a mirror so that when she looks at it she thinks she sees herself, her ring-shaped reflection warped over the outerspace curve of the secret. The reflection in the secret smiles, its mouth says *look at yourself you are so lovely aren't you lovely?* and uses its invisible fingers to dig itself out of her. The fingers hurt where they press. They make the cold fear come but it is no-color. It comes in shapes of feeling instead. Corkscrew and lightening bolt. Thorny trees. Broken teeth. Glass shards. Spikes and forks.

While Edgar's wife opens and closes drawers in the kitchen, Mem closes her eyes and tries to will the fingers away. She holds the secret in. She holds the secret down. She keeps it down like a bile that wants to come out. The bile tastes like chewed-up pancakes, squelchy-sweet. Sticky Ms that won't stay down.

What is she not remembering? There is a message somewhere, its Morse code echo floats through her bloodstream. Mem listens to the teakettle boiling in Edgar's wife's kitchen. The screeching stops. There is a clinking of cups. Mem opens her eyes and sees her half-reflection in the glass covering an old picture of Edgar.

When you're dead, you never have to look at yourself again.

On the day of Edgar's funeral, Mem's mother leaves for a death industry trade show in New York. It begins to snow during a funeral Mem works right before Edgar's, and Mem tries to love the snow, tries to not think the other thoughts but they keep finding her anyway. Mem's wails will have to compete with a tape-recording of Olivia Newton-John's version of *Greensleeves* blaring from a portable boom box held high by the surviving son. After the song is over, the widow fights back tears as she reads a poem by Emily Dickinson, full of tombs and nerves and pain:

This is the Hour of Lead—
remembered, if outlived,
As Freezing persons, recollect the Snow,
First—Chill—then Stupor—then the letting go—

Let it out, let it go. This is what they say to Mem now when she can't stop, patting her on the back as if she has been choking instead of weeping. But there is no letting it go. There is no letting it out. It doesn't ever come out. It is there all the time, shiny and sinuous as a tinsel garland.

Look at yourself. Aren't you lovely?

Now the thoughts have a voice and it finds her, or finds itself inside of her. Mem tries to battle it but it does no good. *No, I'm not,* she tells herself, as she walks through the snow on her way to the next funeral. It is the loveliest snow she has ever seen, long, glass-white crystals brushed by the wind like fur. Across the street, a bundled-up little boy watches his father use an old shoe to scrape the snow away from his windshield. While he scrapes, the father turns to the son and says, "Once this melts we'll see all the dog shit you forgot to get off the lawn." The son wipes his nose on the sleeve of his puffy green coat.

The snow gathers fatly into little skirts around the bottom of Mem's Death March boots. She watches her feet sink into the snow, listening to the rubbery noise. She is a Russian heroine in Siberian exile. The little match-girl on the threshold of death. A lost survivor of some long-ago war. An Eskimo scouting out a new spot for her igloo.

Shut up fucking pig.

The loveliness is gone, wiped aside. Now it is just cold, coming over Mem's fingertips and toes, frightening the blood away like embalming fluid. By the time she is standing behind Edgar's wife, Mem feels like she has no blood left anywhere in her body; even the red crust around her edges feels scraped off like burnt toast. Mem can't help but feel envious of Edgar in his casket. Peaceful. Sewn up. Full of sawdust and nothing. How easy, to just not have to exist anymore. How easy to have other people weeping for you.

Mem herself is tired because of the nightmares. "Everything will be okay," she hears one of the mourners tell Edgar's wife. Everything will be okay, she tells herself, knowing that it is a lie, that she will never be okay. She will never find the magic key. She is worthless. Worse than worthless.

Mem's mother's coffin is being lowered into a hole. Ashes to ashes. Her mother's stitched mouth doesn't say I love you. The mourners are receding now, leaving Mem alone with the casket, the hole, the wind warping the stained canopy.

But something is wrong. The tears won't come. There are whispers and murmurings that slither from beneath handkerchiefs and shawled heads. Mem tries to picture her mother dead but it does nothing.

Mem without her mother.

Nothing comes. She cannot feel like a lost floating thing, a dandelion puff adrift before a storm.

Mem without her mother.

Nothing keeps coming.

Mem without her mother.

The whispers grow fangs.

Edgar's wife turns around, her blanched face imploring.

Mem looks into her mother's coffin but she doesn't see her mother. Instead she sees herself, serene, sewn-up, hands propped across her chest. Mem sees her-

self in the casket and she pulls backward in her mind, away from the casket, to see who has come to attend her funeral. But there's no one there.

Now that Mem can see the site better she notices that her casket is made of flimsy chipboard, the cheap kind that undertakers keep in the basement instead of the showroom. Her makeup is smeared on, the face of a child playing dress-up. The stitches in between her lips are black and jagged. Small welts pout up around each stitch.

Something is under Mem's ribs, trying to push its way up. She covers her mouth with her handkerchief and doubles over. It falls back down, pushes and falls, pushes and falls again. She drops the handkerchief and falls down herself, onto her knees. She holds both hands over her mouth but that doesn't work; that only covers the spit and snot, not the sound.

Yes, yes, that's it. She is in it now, swept up in the sticky waves of it, it has her, it throws her down and beats her. *All your fault, all your fault,* it says, and she knows it is true.

Edgar's wife smiles.

It rolls over Mem. It rolls Mem over, around and around, a morsel on its forked tongue. Something new has come over her. Something else. She can't tell what it is; she is overcome.

I'm sorry! she sobs. *I'm sorry, I'm sorry, I'm sorry!*

She sobs, she falls, she sob, she falls, and she knows that something is wrong. She won't be able to make it out again this time. She won't be able to get it out. She has to find a way to stop it. She can't live like this another day, another moment. She presses her hands against her chest, and her lungs stop seizing, her mouth, still open, grows silent. There is a short breeze and the loose leaves on the hedge lining the cemetery clap wildly, their applause the only noise at the site besides the sound of mourners watching, the sound of Mem trying to breathe.

— 1752 A.D., NORWICH, ENGLAND —

From C.P.W. to M.L.P., a Young Weeping Maid
on Witnessing Her Remarkable Abilities
During the Burial of an Acquaintance

* * *

Soft rain so sweet, her tears divine,
the glittered fringe from soul to eye
were she to shed for me and mine
then I would gladly rush to die.

So grieved am I at graveside when
her trembling tearlets rouse and drop.
Though no good man I know is gone
when she begins I cannot stop.

Behind her veils, a paradise
(were ever I to be so bold)
but sure my love will not suffice
unless it's paid in sacks of gold.

And thus, since I have none to reap
and lo my pocket's poorly fed,
the comely maid who's paid to weep
will only love me once I'm dead.

12

"Did you ever resent your mother?"

Mem is fifteen years old when she realizes that she will never be able to live a normal life. She begins to covet other children's ordinariness, their primary-colored and uncluttered lives, their deathless existences. The children in her neighborhood seem burnished with the grime of outdoor activity. When their mothers call them they run home over the islands of concrete and grass, forsaking treasures of rocks encrusted with mica and onion grass bombs and things rescued from gutter grates. They scatter without the fear of falling or the fear of getting lost, without knowing anything about death except the temporary swooning and falling involved in their war games. *Bang! You're dead!* When they hear their mothers' voices calling, they get up from being dead and run or skate or pedal faster before the court island lights turn on. Playing cards snap in the spokes of their wheels. Abandoned balls bounce on the blacktop.

Mem tries to imagine the soft pink mouths of the other mothers shrieking awful things, sounds shaped like her mother's mouth, the wide eyes and bursting face. The terrible words. *You're a selfish fucking pig.* It doesn't fit, these words coming out of those salmon-shaded lips, that noise coming from the mothers that Mem watches as they call for their children or bring in the groceries or water their squat, ugly shrubs.

These other mothers aren't pretty. They have paunches and short hair the color of dirt or sand. They wear khaki shorts that reveal sunken knees and purple veins, button-down tops that conceal breasts and all hint of breast. Mem imagines them making dinner, soft mothers who check their daughters' homework after the dishes are done. Mothers who tuck them in at night. Mothers who don't scream.

(Later in life Mem will learn other people's houses are never what they seem. Mem will realize that there are no safe homes. She will watch daughters at gravesides, holding tight to their mother-pain like old women clutching handbags. She will remember imagining the rosy mouths of other mothers screaming and wonder, watching the grieving daughters still waiting for forgiveness, *What did she do to you?*)

When Mem walks to the sites the other young Wailers and their mothers whisper and defer to her, the way they used to do for her mother. They all want to shake her hand or ask for advice. She never knows what to tell them. She smiles and shrugs, twists her handkerchief, wishing they would all leave her alone.

At one job, a mausoleum site featuring Mexican *osario*-style encrypt-ment, an over-eager novice asks her, "What do you do when you feel like it's not going to come that day?" She is snub-nosed and freckled, with squinty eyes and a secondhand doole.

"I don't know," says Mem. "I guess, just like everybody else. I impro-vise." She doesn't tell them the truth. She doesn't say, *I picture myself dead. I wish I was dead. I see myself dead with a mouthful of dirt.* But these thoughts are less opaque than usual, and Mem finds another, new thought hiding behind them. It says, *A Master knows how to spend her self, drop by drop, creating a moment that cannot be kept or repeated. My fees are among the highest, my dooles are the finest, and there isn't a woman among you who can approach me. I'm the legend you'll never be.* She turns to look at her mother. *Never.* It occurs to her that this is true. It could be true. She will make it true so that her mother's talent will be seen as mediocre compared to her own. Her mother looks slightly soft now, the flag of black hair less vibrant. How easy it would be to edge her right out of the top position. Mem decides she will do this. She will eclipse her mother with her tears and then leave her behind.

But then her mother's new softnesses and dullnesses send pangs of guilt shooting through Mem's gut. She knows she can never leave. She will never escape. How could she leave her mother? Her mother would never survive such a betrayal. What kind of daughter is she to even think such things? Selfish, shameful, cruel.

Just before the burial, the surviving daughter hands Mem her dead mother's handkerchief to use. When it is the right time to cry Mem presses the faded pink cloth to her face and to her it smells of mothballs and perfume, not like childhood, not like the cookies after school or the anger or the limp bosom or the drunk Sundays after church, or any of the memories this daughter might have of her mother. The perfume is strong and musky. It reminds Mem of nothing.

— SENATE BILL 7001 —

1989 A.D.

THE GENERAL ASSEMBLY OF PENNSYLVANIA

SENATE BILL

No. 7001 Session of 1995

INTRODUCED BY DEPAUL, RIEN, I., PETERS, JORDAN, ELLIOT, BARNETT, O'RIORDIAN, MASH-YOMPOLSKY, GREEN, MARK, JEFFEREYS, WATERS, ADRIAN AND NORTH, JANUARY 23, 1987

SENATE AMENDMENTS TO HOUSE AMENDMENTS, MARCH 19, 1989

AN ACT

Amending titles 18 (Crimes and Offenses) and 42 (Judiciary and Judicial Procedure) of the Pennsylvania Consolidated Statutes, providing for the solicitation, support, hiring, and performance of acts of public mourning.

The General Assembly of the Commonwealth of Pennsylvania herby enacts as follows:

Section 1: Title 18 of the Pennsylvania Consolidated Statutes is amended by adding a section to read:

1 § 626.3 OPEN LEWDNESS by which a person is HIRED to perform any lewd act which he
2 knows is likely to be observed by others who would be affronted or alarmed, or
3 otherwise engages in PROFESSIONAL MOURNING as a business, or displays or causes
4 or permits the display of any lewd act or materials; or loiters in or within
5 view of any PUBLIC PLACE for the purpose of being hired as a PROFESSIONAL
6 MOURNER; knowingly hiring of a PROFESSIONAL MOURNER for FUNERALS or any other
7 PUBLIC DISPLAY OF MOURNING designed to produce an ILLEGAL AUDIENCE; the sale,
8 distribution, delivery, dissemination, transfer, display or exhibit to others, or
9 who possess for the purpose of sale, any book, pamphlet, slide, photograph,
10 videotape, computer depiction or any other material soliciting the SERVICES of a
11 PROFESSIONAL MOURNER; the EXPLOITATION of a child under the age of 17 years by
12 being made to engage in a prohibited act of PUBLIC INDECENCY or obscene and other
13 prohibited public performances; controlling, managing, supervising or otherwise
14 keeping, alone or in association with others, a PROFESSIONAL MOURNING BUSINESS; .
15 procuring, encouraging, inducing, or otherwise INTENTIONALLY causing another to
16 become or remain a PROFESSIONAL MOURNER; leasing or otherwise permitting a place
17 controlled by the actor, alone or in association with others, to be regularly
18 used for the business of PROFESSIONAL MOURNING, or failure to make REASONABLE
19 EFFORT to abate such use by ejecting the PROFESSIONAL MOURNER from the site,
20 notifying law authorities, or other legally available means; a person, other than
21 the PROFESSIONAL MOURNER or his child under the age of 17 years or other legal
22 dependent incapable of self-support, who is knowingly supported in whole or
23 substantial part by the proceeds of PROFESSIONAL MOURNING; soliciting, receiving,

13

"Did you know it was against the law?"

"Don't worry, it'll blow over," Mem's mother says, waving her hand at the air as if that might help it blow over faster. "We just need a few more mushy Democrats in the Senate. We went through this in the eighties when that DePaul schmuck was first elected, and people paid more than ever. They didn't even bother showing up at the sites for the burials, they just sent money orders and let us be. I'm telling you, listen to me. Don't worry. Don't worry!"

At first, business is barely affected. Although the freshly widowed are never good negotiators, they seem willing to pay even more for Mem's services. *How dare they take our grieving rights away from us?* they fume, channeling genuine survivor's anger and sorrow into their new scofflaw angst. *In fact, I'll pay double for your risk. Screw them.* A few months later, there seems to be less and less money available to hire mourners, or at least this is what the funeral directors say. Even Hector is having trouble finding jobs for Mem or her mother. Mem and Sofie overhear their mothers discussing *the recession*, something so bad that Derasha and her mother have had to move to California, to try their hand at the trade there. So far they haven't had much luck. Mem hears her mother telling Aunt Ayin that the mourners there are *in touch* with their feelings and would rather do the job themselves. Binah has to work as a waitress and a cleaning lady, since she has no skills besides wailing, and Derasha has realized that the chicken and steak that she eats are made of dead bodies like the dead bodies in the caskets. Now she won't eat any meat, she keeps getting thinner and thinner and has developed large black circles under her eyes. One night Binah finds Derasha alone in her bedroom, stuffing wads of paper into her mouth.

Mem wants to feel sorry for them but she can't.

When she is in the city with her mother, Mem notices how poverty-stricken, almost homeless, everybody looks now in their dirty and torn clothes. Even the people wearing new shoes or getting out of nice cars are wearing soiled thermal underwear that you can see through the unraveling moth-holes of their sweaters. Knees poke through ripped jeans or shredded stockings. Boys let their tufty, unkempt beards grow in, as if they can't afford to shave. Their hair is greasy and stringy as dirty girls' hair. They say strange things, their words obscured by deep fogs of smoke. *No, dude, aren't you listening? It's the* archetypal *sugar packet.*

The girls look as filthy and impoverished as the boys, except for their flawlessly blackened eyes and carefully lined lips. Their hair isn't feathered into swans' wings or puffed up into some crème-filled dessert. Instead it is flat, shiny, with blunt-cut bangs and raggedy bottoms. The girls poke their fingers through the holes in the cuffs of their sweaters and smoke, languorously. Their fingernails are painted black. But instead of being ashamed for looking so poor, they all seem very comfortable with—even proud of—their rags and tatters. None of these girls look as if they might die of their *squalor.* They are flaunting their squalor, their stained and pilled sweaters, their untied bootlaces, their mysterious half-peeled layers. Even their hungry boniness looks chic to Mem, whose own clothes are even and clean and hole-free. She looks at the neatly pressed cuff of her blouse and wishes she could stick her fingers through it like a fingerless glove.

Mem is supposed to meet Aunt Raziel later that week for dinner at a Chinese restaurant, and now she's sorry she accepted the invitation. She has never eaten Chinese food before and doesn't know what to wear; almost everything she owns is black. She no longer yearns for a pink dress. Now she wants some scuffed black boots, a thermal T-shirt, a checkerboard flannel, and black eyeliner.

Because of the recession, Mem won't be getting any of these things. Mem's mother is already working twice as hard for half her regular fees to make ends meet. This means that there are lots of trips away. It also means that Aunt Ayin has to come along on those trips, since there is twice as much work and Aunt Ayin has no other way to make money during the recession.

While her mother is gone, Mem works several sites alone. The pumpkins displayed around the neighborhoods near the cemeteries have started to soften from the unseasonable heat, toothy jack-o-lantern smiles sagging as flies flit in and out of clumsily cut eye sockets. The trees fringing the cemetery Mem works one Thursday are stubborn and still green, not yet inking their leaves into luscious colors or dropping melon-crimson-amber shawls onto the ground. Some of the leaves have just started to rust and fall from the drought. Once on the ground they shrink up and dry into crunchy brown curls on the side of the road, a thousand boxes worth of cornflakes without milk.

Mem looks at the leaves and tries to hear the sermon given for a man who died while dressed in his wife's best cocktail gown. She learns, listening to the gravelly voice of the preacher under the tent, that even holy men wandering into the Divine Orchard of Paradise in search of secrets go blind, go mad, cut themselves into ribbons, or die. She has also learned that the things people say at funerals have little to do with the true story of the deceased's life and more to do with the parts the survivors can remember, the parts they want to remember, a patchwork quilt of carefully selected memories sewn on top of a life, pieces of stories on top of a whole truth. *He was the best father in the whole world. He lived each day with grace and dignity. He had great taste in clothes.*

On the way to meet Aunt Raziel for dinner, Mem stops at the curb to wait for the red light to change. Across the street, a large group of people her own age are silently staring and laughing at her. All of their eyes are trained on her, fixed and determined. Mem stares right back but they won't look away, they just keep smiling their sarcastic smiles and gaping at her as if she were a sideshow freak. She doesn't know what to do. What is wrong with her? Why is she so weird, so disgusting? She is humiliated. She is furious. She wants to shout across the street, *What are you looking at? Do you know who I am? I'm a legend!*

It isn't until Mem hears a loud *click*! to her left and watches the group dissolve into hearty chatter that she realizes the teenagers have been posing, smiling at someone who is standing right next to her, holding a camera.

Mem walks through the electric orange archway of the China Moon and darts quick looks at all of the well-dressed people sitting in the booths. She can sense the other customers whispering and nudging one another and laughing at her. Many of them are wearing black, too, but Mem knows that her doole is the wrong kind of black dress. She sees Aunt Raziel sitting in one of the booths at the back of the restaurant. She is wearing a long black leather skirt and a purple top, her heart-shaped sunglasses and high heels, a few clip-on lengths of fake jet-black hair pinned in place to hide her bald spots. She doesn't care what anyone thinks or says. Why can't Mem be like that? Why does she care if everyone stares and points? Why are people still staring at her now, as she sits down onto the shiny maroon booth cushion? What is she doing wrong?

The restaurant is decorated with happy, squinting half-moons, hanging paper lanterns, and huge watercolors of mountainsides and rivers. "They have the best pu-pu platter around," says Aunt Raziel. The menu is bright red, laminated, and filled with exotic things Mem has never heard of. *Spare ribs. Egg roll. Shrimp toast.* She hopes that none of these things look the way they sound.

When Mem starts to feel the corrosive rays of someone looking at her, she peers above her menu for a second. She can tell that as soon as she averts her eyes, the someone will start staring at her again. People are always looking at her, but they don't see her the way you would normally see someone. They see her close up and magnified, like the reflection in her mother's mirror with the ping-pong ball bulbs, and they can do more than just see her; they can reach out and touch her close-upness, her too-white skin, the loose thread dangling from the bottom of her skirt.

"So what looks good?" asks Aunt Raziel.

This close up they can see that under the skin Mem is grotesque, deformed, like the children of beggars whose limbs have been wrenched off on purpose. When Mem walks through store aisles she becomes magnified and at the mercy of strange mental pokes and fingerings from other customers and the workers behind the counters. They are all digging for something.

The pu-pu platter turns out to be a miniature tabletop barbecue surrounded by wooden skewers speared through all different kinds of food. Everything has a slice of canned pineapple and an artificially red colored cherry speared at the top. In an almost-whisper, Aunt Raziel tells Mem that all of this food is already cooked through. "But it's the fun of it," she says, smiling.

Mem has to pee, but she knows she can't walk across this room. She won't be able to take it, the eyes will peel her away from herself. Her features will begin to swell, their edges dissolving till she becomes mouthless and featureless, the face of a statue covered in snow. As she sits she feels the air touching her skin and knows there is almost nothing between herself and the rest of the world, she can't tell where she begins or ends. She is an inside-out and boundless body of gelatin, her own veins for tentacles, nerve endings flat, pulsating bouquets sucking at the air. Little black holes. Satellite dishes receiving and receiving. Too much. Too loud. Receiving and receiving.

"You don't like the pu-pu?" Aunt Raziel asks. "Eat more—you're so thin I can see through you."

What is Mem receiving? She can't tell. The someone-else, the ghost-turned-to-armor squatting in her head, gets the messages and relays them: *they hate you ugly disgusting talking too much stupid worthless why aren't you ashamed ashamed hide go hide coward look at yourself you can't even cross a room to pee.*

Raziel bites into her slippery shrimp toast with relish. "Ah, this is the best one," she says.

At the end of the meal a shy Chinese waitress takes the pu-pu platter away and brings a plate of sliced oranges and cookies that look like hard dumplings. "These are fortune cookies," Aunt Raziel explains. "Open it up—there's a fortune inside."

Aunt Raziel's cookie has two fortunes inside. Mem uncrosses her legs to take some pressure off her bladder and carefully cracks her cookie open. Her fortune says: *Follow your dreams,* with a happy face instead of a period.

Mem is disappointed. She doesn't want to follow her dreams. She wants to outrun them, trick them into thinking she is somewhere else, slip around a corner and watch them chase someone else by mistake. She can't follow her dreams; they follow her. She can't escape them.

"What does yours say?" asks Aunt Raziel and Mem hands it to her.

Look at yourself. Look at yourself. All Mem can do is look at herself. All of the time, through the eyes of other people. Their faces are mirrors. Everything is a mirror. Floor-to-ceiling funhouse mirrors, framed with cackling faces.

"Ah, you got a good one," says Aunt Raziel, nodding seriously, placing her two fortunes on the table.

"Are yours good?" asks Mem.

Aunt Raziel shrugs. "I don't know. I don't really believe these fortunes." She laughs, showing all of her yellow teeth.

She looks Mem in the eye and stops laughing.

"You're going to have to make your own fortune, Mem," she says. "You've been given a lot of challenge. No one is going to help you or save you. You're going to have to do it yourself."

Mem nods, picks up Aunt Raziel's crumpled fortunes from the tabletop, a glass square on top of a red-and-gold pattern of China moons.

Your secret desire to change your life will soon manifest.

Let go of what is troubling you.

She will not let herself cry in front of Aunt Raziel. She will not cry here, in public, in front of all of these people who are already watching and waiting for her to fuck up. "You have to get out of the business," says Aunt

Raziel. She fishes through her imitation snakeskin purse for a cigarillo. One of her hair pieces comes loose and sweeps into the crumbs on the table.

"I don't understand," Mem says.

"You are not a stupid girl," Raziel says, looking up. "You understand. It is enough, already, that such a little *maidella* like you is made to live the old life so hard. This world is not the same as it was. It is enough. You have mourned enough. That mama of yours was taught too hard herself, she is made to be hard, but inside her is like you. It is enough for her, too. For both of you. You have to get out of the business." She pulls out a wrinkled bill and puts it on the table for the waitress. She readjusts her hair, snaps her purse closed. "If she won't let you go you will stay with me. I teach you the other trade, then you never have to do this crying again."

Mem is staring at her ragged cuticles, her short fingers lying crookedly in her lap. She cannot look up. This is what she has wanted to hear all along. She has been waiting her whole life to hear it, but she knows if she says anything she will start to cry.

It seems Raziel knows this, too. "You don't have to say nothing," she says quietly. "You might even be angry for me to say anything bad against your mama. I understand this. But I am watching you turning into a ghost more every year. You don't have to be a ghost, Mem. You don't even have to be a Wailer just because you can do it so good. You go home, you think about it. I will be always where you know I am, with the dogs waiting. If you don't come, that is okay, too.

"But don't cry now. Don't cry at home. Don't cry no more," she says, patting her small dark hands on top of Mem's small white ones. "It's *genyck* already. It is enough."

— 1500 B.C., EGYPT —

HIEROGLYPHIC TEXT [FRAGMENT]
Author Unknown

Lament

mother I am leaving

. . . this mourning gown is but a flesh...

I cannot [remove it]. it is ruined even before

I arrive, this weeping they have paid for

this...girl [among] the ashes

. . . .

my blacks and weeds...are destroyed by [sadness]

the papyrus has [feathered] its edges

like linen worn too well but...brittle. I touch the soft fringe softly

as I read of your

...demise...a sudden

taking away from us and the sickle-shaped

mark...an invitation

[to] grieve, a request

for audience. at my table the cosmetics

cover me, I am a porcelain doll, but [I]

am not breakable. I will

appear to break, to peel [and] fall apart like the delicate shell

of an egg...

14

"How does a Wailer get out of the business?"

One morning, after an extremely lucrative funeral in New Jersey, a woman with dry clots of purple lipstick scattered around her mouth follows Mem out of the cemetery, saying that Mem is worse than a stripper, more dangerous than a whore. "A woman being paid to cry in public is the opposite of a celebration of femininity. Do you actually think this is natural?" she asks, verging on shrieking. "Do you think that this is art?" Mem is stunned and doesn't know what to say. Unlike her mother, Mem doesn't think of her work as art. She just thinks it is her job.

But Mem understands why the woman is upset. She is not the first one to accost Mem in this way. Mem knows what these women see when they look at her crying: decades of corseted ladies mixing batter or martinis, girl babies being pulled out of mothers and smashed against rocks. Bound feet, double-veils, iron masks, the Rule of Thumb. Breast implants, high heels, vaginas sewn up like Thanksgiving turkeys.

The 1900s, her mother tells her, have been a bad century to work in the funeral arts because it is simply not in fashion anymore. Maybe it would have been easier if they had only been born a hundred years or so earlier, when scores of Sin-Eaters and Mimes and doole-makers ran businesses in the industry, too, when there were so many other paid theatrical performers hired to work at memorial services and parades. The Mimes were the wealthiest, paid to wear wax portrait masks of the deceased as they mocked the beloved's walk and gestures so that it would look as if the soul of the dead had magically rematerialized for the affair. Then there were the low-end jobs, like the Sin-Eater, an impoverished pariah paid to ingest the sins of the corpse by eating a loaf of bread and a bowl of beer over the dead body. It was a degrading job, because no matter what kind of person the Sin-Eater really was, the rest of the world could only see him as a depraved but necessary social evil, a man so low on the hierarchy that he was willing to doom himself to hell for a living. But what if, Mem wonders, the Sin-Eater didn't believe in sins, or hell, or eternity? What if he was just a secretly wise man who had figured out a way to get paid to eat free food by profiting from other people's fears?

Either way, everyone considered the Sin-Eater unclean. He was so disgusting that even the bowls he used were destroyed after he left the house. This is how Mem feels the week she begins to make her plans to leave. Unclean, disgusting, depraved, and perhaps doomed. But she also feels, for the first time in many years, a thin flicker of hope. The day before her mother leaves for the 1995 death industry trade show in Nevada, Mem watches her mother pack and plans her own escape. She has already put a few things into a plastic shopping bag and hidden it under her bed, although she has no clear idea of what she should take. Underwear, deodorant, a tube of cherry-flavored Chapstick, these things made sense when she put them in the bag, but she doesn't know how many dresses she should take. She had thought she should leave them all behind since she won't be needing them anymore, but what else will she have to wear besides a few button-down shirts and the one pair of jeans?

"I'll be back Thursday. Don't forget to keep at least one light on in the house when you go out to fool the thief," Mem's mother says. Mem looks down at the neatly lined stacks of black dresses. Her mother has been keeping lights burning in the house when she leaves for as long as Mem can remember, always to *fool the thief.* As if there is only one thief, robbing every dark house in the neighborhood, year after year. Mem pictures the thief: short, a cartoon wearing all black, a ski mask, gloves, hunched over in the half-light, listening for noises. Mem sighs, flopping onto the couch with a dramatic flourish. "Whatever," she says.

In the half-second it takes for her mother to whip around, Mem hears the *whatever* echoing in her mind and is suddenly aware of how the bones in her body have draped themselves in an inappropriately blasé pose against the coffee-colored faux-suede cushions. She scrambles to right herself, to make her body more compact.

"Whatever," her mother repeats. She makes *oink oink* noises, scrunching her face up into a snout. "Who the fuck do you think you're talking to? I'm working myself sick trying to scrape up enough money to feed your ungrateful ugly mouth."

Mem feels her own face scrunch up, snout-shaped, and un-called tears come out of her. Mem's mother watches Mem cry for a minute, not softening. Then she turns her back and waves a distracted hand at her daughter.

"You're such a fucking crybaby," she says. "I'm just trying to save our lives here. I love you."

It is enough, Mem tells herself, but her own voice saying it in her head is awful. The vibrations coming out of her mouth are ugly. Mem doesn't want to move from the couch, she is frozen, though her mother doesn't seem to be noticing her at all. Mem hears her mother's steps going back and forth from the suitcase to the stacks on the table and the bare flesh of her arms bristles.

When she leaves, Mem thinks, it will destroy her mother, make her mother sad and sorry, Mem will never come back or speak to her mother again. Her mother will find out from someone else when Mem has children, her mother will eat herself alive with guilt, but Mem will never return. She will wake every morning and put on a coat and step out onto the fire escape with a cup of coffee while the dogs beg to be walked. She sees herself on the balcony, the cup of coffee steaming beautifully, her face calm and poised with a radiation of beatific presence. But with this image comes a second one, the image of the moment after, Mem's sun-lit glow suddenly snuffed out, leaving her small and strange on a filthy fire escape, pretentiously holding a cup of coffee she doesn't even like to drink. She will still be living a lie. She will still be trapped inside of who she is. She could leave her mother but she will never be able to leave herself behind.

She will never be able to escape.

At that moment Mem cannot escape from the couch. She keeps her body tight, still, wishing she could be more shadow than skin. Something is wrong with her ears. She can hear her mother walking from room to room, opening and closing drawers, but there is a high humming static layered over this, like the noise from a refrigerator or a radio between stations, a frantic secret whispered too loudly.

It is enough. It is enough. Isn't it enough?

Mem's mother calls out from her bedroom, "Bring some scrap paper from the kitchen, will you?" Mem heaves herself up from the couch, searches the top kitchen drawer, slowly, sifting through the rubber bands and stray coupons for a pen. She finds paperclips, several packs of almost-used-up matches, and a set of bright yellow plastic corncob holders. She finds a stack of folded scrap paper underneath a pair of broken scissors and a pencil without an eraser. The metal tube that used to hold the eraser is chewed closed and part of a National Organization for Women sticker is wrapped around the other end.

When Mem opens the folded paper she sees that it is not scrap paper at all. It is a pile of computer-printed pages from Jefferson Hospital with her mother's false name on the top, and a pamphlet full of pictures. At first the pictures look like pressed flowers with crushed petals and yawning holes where the centers should be.

The sheets of paper from the hospital are about *cancer*. Above the pictures are descriptions of different kinds of cancer, but they don't look anything like crabs. They are watery lilac sacs and domes. Mangled purple pinwheels. Pretty blisters of paint from an accidental splatter. If Mem didn't know better she'd have thought that this was art.

Mem knows about cancer. She's mourned for its victims. She's seen stories about it on the TV, bald children, emaciated men. Women with various pieces of themselves cut out and sewn up, their bodies becoming clumsily-stitched pillows or poorly altered garments, the slow, draining death. *D* for *Death. Death Rattle. Death Bed. Death Watch. Death Throes. Dying Breath. At Death's Door. Dying Day.* None of these things could possibly refer to her mother, who is still boundless and huge and impenetrable. On the other side of the pamphlet, under the title Normal Cell Division, the cells are stacked in even, orderly rows, like loaves of bread in the supermarket. Not like willy-nilly sprockets and flat stars. Not like deflated lather and bruised flowers. Not like the other picture, which is what the inside of part of Mem's mother might look like now. A magnified cross-section of her mother, dipped in ink and put on display.

All this time, wondering why her mother has been so angry, Mem had thought it was because of the recession. But it is because of this secret cancer, clots of haywire cells spiraling out with no thought of Mem's mother, growing their mirrored selves over and over like pulpy and rootless weeds.

And Mem knows that it is her fault.

She has done this. She has made her mother sick by being the wrong kind of daughter. Ungrateful, selfish, piggish, disgusting. Mem has tried to be the right kind of daughter, she has tried harder and harder through the years to reach that elusive end but it is not possible, it keeps moving and jumping away from her like a butterfly she is trying to catch, or something attached to her mother's fingers with string. She always knew that at some point this would have to stop. Why keep on doing it if she can never get it right? She only wants her mother to love her.

The static is in Mem's ears, louder than before. It is spongy, heavy, and grows into a space beneath Mem's rib-cage. She folds the papers back together and places them under the broken scissors and the pencil and closes the drawer.

Mem forces her voice to sound normal. "I can't find any paper," she calls. She walks into her bedroom, gets down on all fours by the bed, and pulls out the plastic bag. Chapstick, deodorant, underwear, these things come out in the opposite order of how they had gone in. She places them on the carpet, looks at them, looks at the carpet, the puppet-hair yellow carpet that she has known all of her life. *Mem without her mother.*

"Come kiss me goodbye," her mother hollers from the living room.

Mem without her mother.

She will never be able to leave.

— 348 A.D., JAPAN —

From Lady Etsuko to her daughter, Izumi

THE WAILER'S SONG

Come home daughter
do not gaze too long
into the lakes of other places.
I dreamed last night
your robe was too thin
you were lost in the meadow
there was seaweed in your hair.
Daughter the gems you harvest
while weeping are not worth
even one grain
of my love.
Like the sun even when I cannot see you
I feel you and know you are there.
My heart is a dry sponge without you.
It crumbles but it will once more blossom
when I see your face, feel your tears
wet my sleeves.
Until then know I am the air
and the sun and the earth about you.
Keep to the path if snow falls
and do not adorn your hair.
Daughter if I had wings to send...
Come home.

15

"What happens when you just can't cry?"

Mem's mother is cheerfully beating the sofa cushions and pillows to freshen them up. She has been freshening up the whole house since she came home from Nevada five days ago. All of the surfaces in the house gleam. Mem uses one of her mother's handkerchiefs to polish the empty shelves. All of the things that were on the shelves are now on the floor, awaiting a frenzied buffing from Mem's mother.

"You know what we need, baby? We need a vacation. That's what I think," her mother says between blows.

Mem has never even heard her mother use this word before. Mem looks up from her dusting. "I can't take a vacation right now," she says, speaking a little louder than usual so that she can be heard over the pounding. "Hector has me set up for jobs for weeks."

Her mother tenderly places the pillow she has been beating onto the couch and stands back, as if to inspect it. "I know. But you deserve a vacation, you've been working so hard. Wouldn't you like to go swimming in the ocean, just get away from this weather?" She picks the pillow up and starts smacking it again. "God knows we can afford it now."

Mem is annoyed. Why is her mother disrespecting her work schedule, the expectations of her fans? She puts the handkerchief down and repeats, even louder, "I can't take a vacation right now. It would be unprofessional for me to cancel." She doesn't even know how to swim.

Her mother stops what she is doing mid-punch and looks at Mem. She says, evenly, quietly, "Don't you ever presume to tell me what's professional and unprofessional. You might be making high fees but you're still an apprentice. You better remember whose house you're in, and who the Master is." Then she softens. "If you disappeared to take a vacation, there would be some mystery to it. People would be curious about when you'd return. It's free publicity. It would make you even more of a rare catch."

"But I am a Master already," Mem says. She straightens her posture but can't look her mother in the eye. "All of the Aunts say so. Even Hector says so. That's how we got the job wailing tonight for the famous writer."

Mem looks down at the *chatchkas* by her feet, the perpetually smiling porcelain cat, the thimble from Kansas, a miniature shoe made out of crystal. Whose things are these? They can't possibly be her mother's. Mem has lived her whole life in silent symbiosis with the things on these shelves, but until today she has never really seen them before. They give off an aura of inert permanence. They will be be dug up ten thousand years from now by a team of historic researchers. *They obviously worshipped cats*, the head researcher will say with unquestionable authority. *And very, very tiny feet.*

Mem looks up and sees that her mother is staring at the *chatchkas*, too. Maybe she is wondering the same thing, how these objects might still be here years after both Mem and her mother are buried. That these objects are silly and unrepresentative of such an important and serious life. On the outside, her mother's body looks the same to Mem, robust, fertile, multiple. An articulate and ambrosial body, still surrounded by a radiance eclipsing all others. But Mem knows what is growing underneath.

"I guess you're right," her mother says, absently replacing the pillow. "We should both get ready." She turns and walks away into her room.

Mem continues her polishing. After a few minutes, Mem abandons the shelves and goes to her mother's room. She finds her mother sitting primly on the edge of the bed, wearing her late-autumn doole, barefooted, immobile as the porcelain cat. She isn't sure if she should embrace her, or help her put on her shoes. She remains standing in the doorway, unable to move any closer.

"Finish dusting the shelves," says Mem's mother.

The popular novelist they have been hired to weep for was only forty-three when she died last week. She had fallen asleep at the wheel after a late dinner with her agent.

"You just watch," her mother says as they pull up to the site. "Now her latest novel will sell like crazy. Aside from war, nothing is better for business than death." The only famous people Mem knows of are actors from the shows on Aunt Raziel's TV, and other celebrity Wailers like her mother. Several Masters had been vying for this job, but Mem and her mother were offered the highest fees. It is a risk to work such a prominent job since so much attention and publicity could prompt a raid, but there is no way they can refuse. "This is what all the jobs used to be like in your great-grandmother's day," her mother explains as they walk. "Dignity, fashion, romance. And plenty of money."

The cemetery looks like an ordinary cemetery, green and white and gray, but it is clear that it is not going to be an ordinary job site. Men in dark suits and sunglasses stand at each canopy pole, mumbling into walkie-talkies and jerking their heads curtly at each other. Dozens of pure white orchids artfully cascade around the hole in the ground. Mem recognizes four Wailers who step up to stand behind her. Mem offers them each a quick, assertive nod, just as her mother does. Although this is a funeral for a celebrity, Mem feels that she and her mother are the true celebrities, standing statue-stiff and framed by the gray, the whole world waiting for their rain. The arriving mourners look ordinary, too, walking embarrassedly up to the tent, although up close they seem thinner than most people, their edges more well-defined. Eventually the initial coughing and whispering subsides, and the walkie-talkie men step farther away from the crowd, tensely surveying the cemetery as if there are dozens of thieves camouflaged as tombstones, harbored between the cones of plastic flowers, lying in wait.

It is almost time to begin but Mem is feeling too steady, too cleanly spooled, to do the damage she needs to do in order to well up. *It is impossible to be empty and cry at the same time. Just watch the Master nearest to you and emulate.* Sighing, Mem looks up and sees that her mother's face is still dry. Mem thinks this must be the new technique she has heard about, *meditative delay*, the latest way to captivate the mourners by holding back until the last possible moment. It is exactly the sort of dramatic skill her mother enjoys mastering.

But once the nondenominational clergywoman is finished speaking, it is already past the last possible moment. It is the end of the job, and her mother is still dry.

Mem's mother chews at her lower lip, anxiously kneading her tear ducts with her fingertips. She drops her hands, her dry handkerchief fluttering to the Astroturf. She twitches her head toward Ayin and nods, softly. With a briskness Mem would never have suspected she was capable of, Ayin grabs her sister's arm in one hand and Mem's arm in the other and whisks them both past the other Wailers, vigorously, back to the car.

It must be the cancer, thinks Mem, but she knows she cannot say it out loud. She doesn't even know if Ayin knows. The ride home is silent, leaden, all three staring dumbly out of windows at the endless stream of shopping centers and chain restaurants.

Mem remembers the story of the famous 15th-century Wailer from Yorkshire who was found guilty of treason and slain, her body tossed into a deep ravine on the outskirts of her village and then forgotten. Years later a beautiful tree grew where the Wailer's body had been. It bore an unusual fruit concealed in layers of paper like an onion, and, like an onion, the fruit itself brought tears to one's eyes but became very sweet when cooked. A century ago, the fruit stopped bearing but the tree itself survived. To this day, lovers who sit under the tree find that they cannot kiss, they can only cry. They spill their paper cups of coffee, their once-plump desire shrivels and dies. They cling and muddy the cuffs of their jeans while they whisper and weep and do not know why.

As a small child, whenever Mem heard someone say *over my dead body*, this story was what she thought of. Now she pictures her mother's dead body. But this time it does not glow. Its light has been choked out, drawn out, bled out like juice. What can Mem do? She digs her thumbnail into the skin around her cuticles.

Although Mem cannot remember a time when she wasn't aware that she and everyone she knew would soon die, this illness is still a shock. *Over my dead body.* She has been conscious all her life of not only the idea of death itself, but the knowledge that this moment, any moment she might have in her hands right now, might be the last one before death, that this death will cause suffering first, that there is no afterlife, that this is it, each moment of juice-drinking or bored Sundays or picking dandelions in the backyard is therefore the one-and-only and last time. That every time she sees her mother's mouth, be it smiling with love as it smothers her with kisses or shaping itself into a monster hole as it screams at her, will be the last time.

This funeral is the last time she and her mother will work together. Mem looks up at her mother's hair coiling over the seat in front of her and wants to do the impossible, wants to latch onto the hair and make time stop. But there is no stopping it, nothing stops. The CVS drugstores and T.G.I. Fridays and Staples superstores whiz past the car, mocking Mem with their brightness and regularity. *Her dead body.*

It is not the body itself which makes Mem want to curl up in the backseat and weep. It is this endless glut of highways, these gruesome buildings, the fact that they will all still be here when Mem's mother is gone.

— 20TH CENTURY, UNITED STATES —

Author Unknown

EXCERPT, *About Sjogren's Syndrome*

The central lachrymal gland is positioned between the eye and a superficial dent in the frontal bone. It manufactures the spill of tears caused by shifts in mood, unlike basal tears which are generated continuously, up to ten ounces a day.

Perhaps the most valuable part of the 'reptilian' hindbrain in human emotional response is the *medulla oblongata*, which, in mammals, has evolved networks of lumpy tracts and ridges to create our nonconscious processes. It has been suggested that, due in large part to this recent development in our mysterious gray matter, the first mammalian vocalization was the 'separation cry,' a noise triggered as a response when parent and offspring are separated.

In addition to the flow of emotional tears, the evolution of the weeping human body includes a change in muscle positioning in the eyelids, eyebrows, mouth and forehead. While weeping, the whole of the body is involved: lungs, heart, even salivary glands play their part. As the tears drain through the *puncta* (commonly referred to as tear ducts) to the lachrymal sacs, they flow into channels which empty themselves out into the sinuses. Clusters of neurons fire, the flesh organ flushes. It is an elaborate cooperation that provides the human body with the simple release of tears.

There is a unique disorder which strikes almost 10 percent of the female population in this country, a sudden condition which denies its sufferers even the simple production of work-a-day basal tears. Known as sjogren's syndrome, this degenerative disease can come on suddenly during pregnancy, lactation or menopause, causing a woman's lachrymal sacs to 'dry up' and become vestigial. There are no methods of early detection and no known cure for the syndrome, although most patients are prescribed saline-based eye drops, which they can administer to themselves by hand as needed.

16

"Are older Wailers allowed to retire?"

"I don't know what else I can tell you. They just won't produce," the doctor says, handing Mem's mother a pamphlet.

"Is it some sort of fatigue or paralysis?" Mem's mother asks, but the doctor simply shakes his head. Paralysis was a word suggesting that things might move again one day, that her glands might someday be useful. Fatigue implied that there would be a resurrection. But this nice, round, bespectacled doctor with the white tufts scattered across his crown was telling her the truth: no cure, no therapy, no magic. No wetness.

Mem watches the pamphlet become damp and limp in her mother's perspiring hands.

Throughout Mem's mother's life, the word *Sjogren's* was something you weren't supposed to say out loud. It was forbidden, a bad word, a word powerful enough, once uttered in mixed company, to silence a room. Her own mother had pretended that the disease was a blessing, a sign that she should abandon Wailing and become a trainer, which she had claimed all along was her true calling.

Mem's mother has always believed in callings but she has also always believed that as she aged, she would lose one seemingly indispensable feature after another. But never this. Now her celebrated eyes are waterproof. Now she is a desiccated well, worse than tainted or stagnant, nothing suspended or stifled or withdrawn, not even an emptiness that can be filled.

So this is it after all: the first need on the list of things she will never be able to have again. Now she will be nothing but a dry witness suffering a frustrating constipation. This is the someone-else face she has been fighting against for the past twenty years, the face of her own freeze-dried self in the coffin, cured with salt. Here it is, the beginning of uselessness and embalmment.

Even bad water is better than none at all. This was one of the first lessons she had learned. She had memorized it dutifully almost a half-century ago, but she was very little then and didn't know what bad water was. She had imagined a mischievous sludge sneaking out of a well to wreak havoc on the neighborhood. A glass of water being scolded by her mother.

Mem looks hard at her mother sitting on the bed after they return from the doctor's office. Mem says, firmly, "It will come back."

Mem's mother's face is blank but she radiates longing. She nods, uninspired, and stands up, unbuttoning the side of her doole. Her emanations are as blank as her face, a blanket of TV static loud as the static in Mem's ears, to cover up the real noise beneath it. "You're right," she says. "It will come back."

Mem twists her fingers together church-and-steeple style while she watches her mother undress. She knows what her radar is registering now. It is a make-believe signal, something designed to trick the receiver. It is a drowsy surrender with edges of rage. It is the apocalypse coming, insurrection, a plague. Growing up, Mem had heard several stories told about a Wailer in ancient China who was able to time her pattern of crying and stopping to match the rhythm of the mourning drums. In the one surviving drawing of her, now hanging in a museum in France, she is depicted sitting in a corner, lost in the folds of her white robe, surrounded by gifts of crimson eggs wrapped in red ribbon, pots of plum jellies, and platters of pork ovaries. She was loved not for her tears but for her control, the musical throb and halt, the breathless pauses, the true gift: not the crying, but the stopping. The sign of a Master. But the stopping is only considered a gift if, once stopped, the Wailer can start again. Stopping for good used to

mean banishment; in the old days Mem would have been expected to liq-
uidate her mother's assets and send her off, or pay to have her killed in a
painless and honorable way.

"It will come back," Mem says again, though she doesn't believe this.
Fearful and awed into a rare silence, Aunt Ayin tries to find a cure. She
scatters handfuls of sacred salt from the *Via Salaria* in Rome across Mem's
mother's patchy lawn and inside of the house, watching the grains bounce
across the linoleum. *To absorb evil vapors.* She lights red candles and writes
Mem's mother's name on the wall with invisible inks. She brings in a drum
made of snakeskin to ward off all creeping things. She rubs Mem's mother's eyes with sapphires, chants and hangs suspensions, picks runes and
burns smudge and cooks Secret Confections. She makes Mem's mother eat
dry host biscuits baked with salt and drink flower-essence elixirs. Aunt
Ayin believes that all Mem's mother needs is a healing balm, an anoint-
ment, something young and made of water. A matrix that can unclog
Mem's mother's plumbing and begin the process of distillation. Mem's
mother does not resist. She has already resigned herself to this new fruit-
lessness and has stopped fighting. On the newly glossed refrigerator, next
to the shopping list, is a paper covered in Aunt Ayin's alchemical symbols:
solution, sublimation, to rot, to anneal, to purify, quintessence, time,
water, work complete.

Her mother begins to talk in her sleep. Even with her bedroom door
closed, Mem can hear her mother asking in a clear, loud voice from her
room *Where do you keep your glasses? I don't trust a room without windows. I
said that would be fine, didn't I? Who painted these tables?*

"We should have seen the signs," Aunt Ayin says. She brings out a
deteriorating leatherbound book.

"Here are the warnings," she reads.

A white rose in autumn.

Dropping a mirror in which you have seen your reflection.

Ebbing tide.

Spiked leaves.

Fruit and flowers on the same tree.

— 842 A.D., CHINA, T'ANG DYNASTY —

Written by an Unnamed Courtesan of the First Order
Translated by Micah Volk

She
weeps alone
caged by
waterfalls
of light.
Outside
the mourners
ruin the moss
with their waiting
and
children
crowd together
like blossoms
on a branch.

Does she
see
the thousand rivers
that pass?
Day
and night
she brushes the
strings of her
sorrow
and will not put
a plum
in her mouth.

Soon the men
will come in
to throw
coins
at her feet.
She will
break then
as a cracked
pitcher,
her soul
emptying itself
to make room
for all the water,
and
all the incense
in all the
houses
will be too
damp to burn.

17

"How can you still love a mother who did this to you?"

The look on her mother's face as she says goodbye when Mem leaves for work one snowy Saturday morning makes a vibrating knot grow in Mem's throat. It is the day before Mem's seventeenth birthday and her mother will spend the day cooking and cleaning and baking Mem's cake. She looks tired, yes, but that isn't all. There is something else, but not the angry someone-else that sometimes inhabits Mem's mother. This new look on her face is the lack of a look. At first, Mem tries to forget the look as she walks through the snow, a thick, clotted snow that covered the trees with pristine cottonballs overnight. But the image of her mother waving goodbye from the doorway, wearing her big, suddenly-too-heavy-looking black coat, the helpless, condemned smile, these gnaw at Mem, irritating and irresistible as the itch from a mosquito bite.

All of the noises in the cemetery are subdued by the snow. Mem hardly hears one of the oldest Aunts as she trudges forward to stand next to her. "We haven't seen your mother in a while," she says. "I hope she's all right."

The Aunt is hunchbacked and skeletal, her face covered in brown spots the size of jelly beans. She has covered her boots in clear produce bags. She smiles at Mem in a concerned, kindly way, but to Mem the sunken eyes seem sickeningly amused.

"She's fine," Mem says. "She's taking a vacation."

Mem has already begun to miss her mother. Her mother's insides are like a missing person, slightly moldering and honeycombed with a powdery desiccation, calcified rime on the brink of collapse. Some vital quintessence has been leached out of her, a cold seep that has left behind a beautiful but brittle cloth. Now Mem's mother is a ruin on display like the relics of Rome Aunt Ayin always talks about, imposing and memorable and only good for looking at. She has begun the ghost-like shrinking, the erosion that she always expected and dreaded. Soon she will be almost transparent, thin and deprived as ice.

Mem sees her own cloaked body below her, stark in its draped black fabric against the snow, and it becomes clear to her that her mother was right, what she is seeing is just a shell, something that can be pried open or husked off by someone-else. She looks at her hand and sees its shellness, turns it over to examine the palm, expecting it to be calcified, or twisted into a nautilus. But it isn't. It is just a hand, a small fleshy carcass that she wishes she could use to cover her face as the old Aunt shuffles back to her place in the rear. "Send her our best," the Aunt calls, her ancient voice reedy and thin in the cold.

At the moment the mourners begin walking toward the gravesite, Mem realizes that soon people will forget that her mother has ever been a Master. The legend will fade out like the end of a TV drama, and all of the other Masters will be thrilled. It might even be cause for celebration, the dethroning of a Wailer who ruled for half a century. Mem wonders what they are already saying, who will take her place in the front, next to Mem.

Mem wailing without her mother.

Mem without her mother.

First there will be whispers, then rumors, then stories. Mem can already hear the unprofessional hags talking by the holes. *I always knew she would wear out some day. Maybe she's been faking it all along. She's damaged goods. She's polluted. She's contaminated. Sure, they say it's Sjogren's but that was her mother's excuse, too.*

That night, at home, Aunt Ayin sits at the kitchen table and pores through her big musty books. "At least everyone will remember you as a Master," she says to Mem's mother. But Mem knows this isn't true. It is the opposite of the truth. For a while they will remember her mother as a fallen woman, a Wailer too big for her britches and knocked down by fate, but eventually they will not remember her at all. There will be no Lessons with her mother's name in them for future generations to memorize. There will be no legend of Celeste. Mem without her mother is one thing, a temporary peculiarity, while the profession without her mother's legend is something else. Someday Mem will die, too, and her grief will go with her. But for Wailing to go on, for the hags to dishonor and forget her mother, this will be a permanent condition. Her legend is a story that will stop being told.

A permanent condition. Even Mem knows that, except for death, there is no such thing.

"You know the Romans took Palestine because they needed to harvest salt from the Dead Sea," her mother says as she ignores Ayin and rubs the refrigerator handles with rags. "If the Romans hadn't been so desperate for salt, the whole Jesus thing would have turned out totally different."

Mem's mother doesn't care about Aunt Ayin's signs. She seems to Mem like she is tired of fighting, tired of thinking about her body, which has now betrayed her twice. Mem knows her mother does not want to live too long, does not want Mem to have to monitor all the solids and liquids that will have to go into her mother's body and all the solids and liquids that will have to come out, to look after bedsores and live with the smell of her flesh slowly going bad, like forgotten leftovers. Perhaps if Mem's grandmother were there, forcing treatment tubes into her arms and down her throat, whacking her in the head with a wooden spoon or flushing her head in the toilet whenever Mem's mother started to drift off, it would be different.

But Mem's grandmother isn't there. There is only Mem, and Aunt Ayin, and a beady-eyed photograph scowling its disapproval from the mantel.

Scouring the stovetop, circling her arm so furiously that the rubbery flesh between her elbow and armpit swings from side to side, Mem's mother says, "It's no surprise that the soldiers were paid in salt. That's where the word salary comes from. Plenty of our ancestors were paid in salt and spices instead of gold, and they didn't mind."

What would the ancestors say?

They'd say: *Accept it, Celeste. Your number is up.*

Go find the list. Who shall we hire?

Curled up in bed, trying to sleep, Mem hears a low-pitched sound come from her mother's room. Mem shifts a little to hear better and the clean sheets rustle under her with a dryness that makes all her hairs stick up.

When Mem was much younger, she had been confused whenever she heard someone say, *so sorry for your loss.* It didn't make sense to her, these two ideas, death and loss paired together. Losing or being lost was an action, a state of being, and death, her mother had told her, was nonaction, no state at all.

But now, as she listens to her mother moaning in the other room, Mem begins to see that going from young to not-young to dying to dead is mostly about loss after all. Hair, teeth, blood, elasticity, strength, all go missing, or evaporate, never to be found again. One by one the organs lose power, the body becomes a shut-down factory with smashed window panes. Then you are just lost. Then your survivors are lost, and lost behind, struggling to find out where they are in a world where their loved one no longer exists. This, Mem realizes, is why she is hired to cry. She is wailing not for the dead but for the people who are still alive, for the loss, the loss, the loss that will never be found.

This sound sliding its way through the hallway from her mother's room is her mother's real crying, sobs popping out like reluctant corks from a bottle, one-two-three-four-five-six and then a breath. It is the breath of someone caught up from drowning, the breath of someone who does not want to be crying. This is not the sound of Mem's mother weeping at funerals. This is unorchestrated, beyond control.

Mem does not want to hear it. She stays in the same position on the bed so that she can hear it, on her side, one leg bent on top of the other, one arm under her head, the other by her face. It is hard to stay in one spot.

The sound coming from her mother makes her want to cry, too, but she won't, she has to stay stiff. "Make it stop," she whispers, but there is no one there to hear and she isn't sure that she really wants it to stop.

What she finds when she finally goes into the other bedroom is her once-beautiful mother wearing a full face of frightening makeup, crying without tears in the closet on top of her shoes. The front of her red silk nightgown is soaked through with snot. When she sees Mem standing in front of the closet she touches a battered pair of old-fashioned pumps that have fallen out of their box by her side.

"I wore these to my mother's funeral," she says.

"I'm sorry," she says.

What can Mem say to this, to her huge and looming all-powerful mother, the strong and starlit mother, the mother who now crouches in her closet dripping clown-mouthed spit onto her best nightgown as she coughs and cries and doesn't get up?

Mem says, "Everything will be okay."

Mem says, "I love you."

She puts her small arms around her mother and feels that her mother has shrunk, feels her sudden fragility, her trembling, smells her sweaty smell and says, "I'm sorry," and begins to cry herself.

For a moment, Mem still needs her mother to be her mother. She lets her mother cradle her, and for a second it feels wrong, bad, like the other times she rocked Mem after making her cry. This feeling passes. Mem closes her eyes and lets herself be rocked. The toes of scrunched-up shoes poke her buttocks and the tops of her thighs in rhythm. Mem feels them and she doesn't care because she already misses her mother. She realizes she has been missing her mother her whole life. She smells her mother's smells and listens to the creak of her bones as they rock in their sockets.

Mem's mother's breathing has slowed now, a tide dragging back in over stones. "Mem," she whispers, "I don't have cancer."

"What?" Mem asks, her voice muffled by the fabric of her mother's gown. She looks up. "Are you cured?"

Mem's mother shakes her head. There are blotches where the makeup has smeared into bruise-shapes on her cheeks and chin. She clears her throat. "No, honey," she says. "I never had cancer. I was never sick."

Mem's mouth drops open. "But the Sjogren's...I went with you to the doctor..."

"The Sjogren's is real, I didn't know it was coming. I must have given myself a *kinaherah*," her mother says, starting to cry again. "But the cancer...I love you so much, I couldn't lose you. I knew you were talking to Raziel. I knew you wanted to leave. I had to do all of this, I did it for you, because I love you."

Mem feels what seems like excitement rising up from her bowels, but by the time it reaches her heart, it has transformed itself into nausea. As she pulls away from her mother her movements seem jerky and convulsive. "How could you do this to me?" she asks, almost whispering. Her mother stops crying and pulls back.

"How could I do this? You made me do this," she says, her voice getting louder. Mem stares at the shoes scattered around them on the closet floor. "If you loved me, Mem, if you really loved me, if you hadn't been so selfish, thinking only about what you want—"

"But you did horrible things!" Mem yells, her voice high-pitched and erratic. "You did this to me! Your mouth did this to me!" She is about to stand up when she hears the phone ringing in the kitchen. In her confusion, Mem thinks that maybe it's Raziel calling to say she knows what has happened, that she is coming right now to Mem's house to get her. Mem breaks free from the tangle of her mother's body and old shoes and races through the house. She answers the phone, out-of-breath, her bare feet icy against the linoleum. It is Aunt Ayin. Mem says hello. She listens. The plastic from the phone turns warm, it feels organic against her face.

"That's not funny," she says, then crumbles to the floor as if she has been kicked.

Aunt Ayin has told her: Aunt Raziel is dead from a stroke. In her makeshift will, written on a piece of stolen hotel stationery, Aunt Raziel has left Mem her television set.

— 2400 B.C., NORTH AFRICA —

Shard from a Sumerian Cuneiform Tablet

APPEAL FROM A DRY MOTHER TO THE GODDESS INANNA

O Inanna, your dirge is nectar.
Your garlands are perfumed, and petals strewn like rain.
Let me call you now!
Lift this curse! If I am not soon ripe again for the howling
wet and prolific as seeds burst from the pomegranate
she will banish me to live among the lepers.

Inanna, hear me! You are terrible!
You are fierce and there are flowers everywhere.
Seduce the water from my eyes
and I will be victorious.

From the palace in heaven
must come the word: Weep
and I know that I am saved.

18

"Have you ever mourned for someone you love?"

In the back of the store where Mem has gone to buy a dress to wear to Raziel's funeral, Mem looks at herself in the dressing room mirror and thinks, *This is ridiculous. She would hate this dress.* She lets her arms hang at her sides. The dressing room smells of feet and corn chips. She hears the people in the store laughing and shopping and checking price tags as if this is just any other ordinary day. As if everything is all right.

We are never supposed to attend the funeral of someone we love, Aunt Ayin said when the girls were still learning. *You will become confused about where your true grief ends and your job begins, or—perhaps worse—lose control and make a spectacle of yourself for free. Instead, schedule yourself for as many jobs as possible and use what you are feeling to fuel your weeping. Genuine grief is a windfall for Wailers. Real tears are worth their weight in gold.*

In the city, the fashion is all-black. Everyone looks as if they are in mourning, even the teenagers slouching under streetlamps, taking moody drags off their cigarettes and mumbling half-bitten comments to their comrades with a clumsy dialect of sulky shrugs and sighs. Their faces are stuck with curls of metal, like shrapnel. They pluck at their brand-new tattoos with crusty fingernails and poke through wreaths of smoke to ask for spare change which Mem does not have.

Other people want her spare change, too. Almost-homeless vendors with their wares spread out on blankets, sidewalks covered in someone else's memories. Sad phantoms curling around steam grates. People pass them by or walk neat ellipses around them, as if they are stray dogs or their condition were catching.

Walking down the street Mem hears a man on a stoop about half a block ahead of her having an animated debate, yelling into his cell phone about the role of American Chinese in institutionalized racism against blacks. He gesticulates, pauses for dramatic effect, even nods, laughing good-naturedly, while allowing his opponent to respond. "Well," he says into the phone as Mem gets closer, "I think you're sorely mistaken," and it is then that Mem realizes he is not speaking into a cell phone at all, but a crushed beer can held against the side of his face. "Listen to what I'm trying to tell you," he articulates into the can as she passes. "I know what I'm talking about." For a second Mem feels sad for him but she quickly realizes that the conversation he thinks he is having is a thousand times more interesting and meaningful than anything she could possibly have to say.

It is strange to be in the city without her mother. Soon, when she can afford it, she will leave her mother forever.

Mem without her mother.

Mem without her.

Mem without.

Mem.

There are throngs of business-suited people standing outside of the skyscrapers, pressed against the walls, appraising their reflections in the windows, smoking cigarettes as if their lives depend on it. Most of these people are wearing doole-black suits, the burly shoulder pads and pouf skirts gone, ripped jeans and dirty thermals nowhere to be found. Now the women look smooth, polished, sleek in their streamlined black jackets and short skirts and artfully upswept hair. They look angry and important. They don't know, Mem thinks, how temporary they really are. None of these women are smiling in their austere black costumes. None of them are wearing patterns. They stare at their own reflections and watch the smoke fan out from between their slippery lips. Their mouths are the only bright things about them, stained the red, orange, or pink of summer flowers, glistening with false lubrication.

As she hurries through the fixed fog of smoke, Mem thinks that maybe these women know what she knows, that patterns are tricks, what you put on top of cheap fabric so you can't see its flimsy grade, like covering rotten meat with spices. Mem is sure now that all patterns are unreliable. If she lets her eyes unfocus for a second she can always find faces on the linoleum pattern in her bathroom at home, maybe a silhouette of bleeding lines, maybe an eye or a smile. But if she looks away and then looks back, the face always disappears.

Birth-death-decay. This is the one pattern Mem knows she can trust. The rest are man-made, an attempt to find—what? Truth? A divine thumbprint? The one pattern that goes on forever? But all patterns break. There is no hidden message. There is only something once forgotten. You only find what you already know.

At the corner, Mem looks up at the traffic light, the red cyclops eye and gaping mouth, the black-clad swarms rushing past her to cross the street. She feels all the movement of the city streaming around her. She covers her mouth and begins to cry.

— 2002 A.D., DELAWARE, UNITED STATES —
Essay, written by Rana Adi, Former Wailer

STICKS AND STONES

At the graves we were only being paid to do what most people do each day for free, reenacting something painful that we did not understand. Imagine if, while stealing or drinking beer or starving yourself or mating with strangers or beating your wife, you were being paid to do this one destructive thing that you couldn't stop yourself from doing anyway. Imagine how skilled you would become. You could raise your compulsion to the status of art form. You could, like us, become celebrities. But to do this you would have to be willing to fall to pieces, and not just once but a thousand times. Yes there were pieces—it was not a façade, we really did break each time we cried, the pieces half-mending themselves back into place before being forced apart again and again.

But how did we do it? This is what most people ask me. I know now that it was the words that came from my mother's mouth that gave me the ability to cry on cue. Once absorbed, all of these words moved through my bloodstream, pumping through the heart and lodging themselves around the body. They were always there whenever I needed them. But they were also there when I didn't, and that was how the problems began. Sticks and stones may break bones but eventually those bones will heal, and the sticks and stones are real things, you can hold them in your hands after they've hurt you and say, "See this stick? See this stone? See my bones? They are broken." There is no mistaking any of these objects, *stick, stone, bone*, but with words you have no proof.

Since I'm no longer a professional, the words that are still there inside of me are well under control, though sometimes one gets loose and cycles its way freely through the system for a while, and when this happens it surfaces in my mind in an uncontrollable way, it flashes there over and over again, the way laundry hits the dryer door as it spins round and round. *Stupid, stupid, I am stupid.* Sometimes this can go on for days. When the other words sense this happening from wherever they are hiding, they dislodge themselves and hook onto each other like a train. Then they can all go round together for a while. *I am stupid. I am worthless. I am disgusting.* Sometimes they change shape or use camouflage—*I am an idiot. I am a failure*—but they do not feel any different. These words are useless now, they did their job, they helped me to make a fortune. But I know they will never come out, I'll be trapped with them for the rest of my life.

19

"Doesn't all this death and gloom depress you?"

Mem dreams of stars pouring themselves vigorously against the sky like a cosmic soda. She dreams her teeth are falling out. She dreams of her mother, sitting alone in a gallery, topless and smoking a cigarette. *What are you doing?* Mem asks. Her mother looks away. *I've only borrowed these tits anyway*, she says, bright white smoke fanning out from between her lips like the cloud-factory smokestacks on I-95. She hands Mem the cigarette and Mem tries to smoke it but every time she breathes in, the fire in the tip goes out. She tells her mother, *I have to get out of here before they find out I don't have a ticket* and her mother answers, *You're the one who was supposed to print the tickets last night, where are they?* Mem remembers that this is true, she was supposed to print the tickets and now everyone will try to get into the gallery without one. She runs out of the gallery and gets into her car, a one-seater that just about fits onto the single-lane luge-rail of the rollercoaster highway. At the top of the highway she realizes that she will either have to drop her car into the river below and then swim out or leave the car there and take the elevator underground to the airport. She only has a few minutes left to go home, print the tickets, and then come back but she has to wait for the ferry to pass before she can do anything. She looks into the rearview mirror and is horrified by how white and plain her face is. She cannot look like this in public. There are hundreds of people coming to this event! She finds her mother's makeup case in the glove

compartment, sealed with plastic that she has to rip off with her fingernails. Mem tries to draw lips on top of her real lips with the liner but it
smears, and when she tries to fix it the whole point breaks off and dangles
from the corner of her mouth. She wipes it all off with a receipt from the
ashtray and tries again, this time without the liner, but when she looks into
her mirror she doesn't see someone prettier. She sees a small, white face
with clown-lips and bright pink doll-blotches on each cheek. Mem tries to
take it off with a receipt but the lipstick is waxy and only smears. She rubs
her mouth, hard, and when she licks her lips she can feel little shreds of
skin. She uses her tongue and teeth to bite and pull and pull them off while
she puts the makeup back into the bag, but it won't all fit in and the plastic wrap has disappeared. The ferry has moved away and traffic is back-
ing up behind her; where did the airport elevator go? It was there a second ago, and now it is dark out, and the people are probably at the gallery.
The dead parts of her lip-shreds don't hurt when she bites them, but each
pull yanks at the spot where the skin is still attached and alive. It hurts but
she pulls anyway. The car tips forward. The shreds taste like metal and
nothing.

In the morning, Mem is too tired to change from her pajamas into her day
clothes. Her mother is not home, so it doesn't matter anyway. She doesn't
have to work until later in the afternoon. In the four months since Raziel's
death, Mem has developed the dishonorable bad habit of not being able to
stop crying. During burials, she has a hard time fighting it off until the
right moment, and then as she works she forgets that anyone else is there,
that she is there. Sometimes she can't keep up with it. It floods up and boils
over, the froth running down the sides of Mem in seething tributaries. The
drips are bitter and eat away at the rest of her, leaving runners and burns
and invisible bruises. When the tears come they don't need to be coaxed
into being anymore. Bitter fingers are already whispering through her
head all day long like the half-memory of a very old nightmare. Now
when the tears come she cannot rein them. They rattle the inside of her
head and buck from her eyes, sloppy, delinquent, and not at all profession-

al. But at least she can still work. Now she saves her money in an old shoe box, instead of handing it over to her mother. Soon she should have enough to leave, although she has no idea where she will go.

At home, the crying is different. It comes cloaked, it stalks her, seething beneath the cloth like a bad molar. It is full of pinholes and miniature petulant mouths, an opus of cavities and ulcers. She hears its chronic shuffle in the hallway, tired and cold and missing her. She can't help herself. Now she wants it. Now she is addicted to it, the taste of salt, the swollen lips, the loss of her own self as it comes gasping into puddles of saltwarm and opened mouths watering. The escape from the attack of one pain into the chrysalis of another. The splintering.

Come, she whispers through the keyhole.

Come, she murmurs through the cracks in the wall. It sheds its bastard fur in the hallway, mouthlike pores dilating for the nipple. There is honeysuckle at the door. There are bowls of meat at the door. There are strings playing and bread baking at the door.

She sits in the corner and crouches to the floor and calls again and calls.

Come, she croons.

Come, she says.

Come, she calls.

And it does.

Mem is so hungry. Her body feels as if it is eating itself alive from the inside out. There is plenty of food in the house but Mem can't be bothered to prepare it. She opens the refrigerator door, sees the carton of milk, and knows that making herself a bowl of cereal will require a gargantuan effort. Just imagining this laborious and many-stepped process is exhausting. It will be easier to not eat at all.

Mem also suspects there is a good chance that she will start crying while she is eating. She knows from experience that crying while eating is an almost impossible thing to do. The two activities are at extreme cross-purposes, one focusing on something going inside and the other on something coming out, and the risk of this happening today is too great because the weeping doesn't go away anymore, not even while she goes to the bathroom or tries to eat.

Mem returns to her room and curls up in bed, knowing that unlike most anywhere else in the house, under the sheets is a safe place to be. She locks her body together like a jaw but finds she can't sleep this time. She sits up and the corner of her contour sheet pops off and creeps down the plastic mattress cover. Mem looks at it and gets out of bed, pulling a sweater on over her pajamas, which are beginning to smell sweetish, the smell of Mem asleep.

Filthy. Smelly. Lazy.

The voice inside Mem slurs as she tries to wash her face, slowly rolling the bar of soap between her heavy hands. It whispers from behind the shower curtain, from inside the closet, from under the dust-ruffles. The voice is full of bile and pus. It is not Mirabelle. It doesn't sound like Mem. It sounds like Mem's mother, the mouth of Mem's mother, trapped inside of Mem.

"Shut up," Mem says, weakly.

But it will not shut up. It prowls around inside of her, softening and sickening and split, oozing like old tomatoes while she tries to tie her shoelaces. Outside the front window she sees that the snow is melting, rushing into the sewers by the islands, dragging cigarette butts and pota-to-chip bags and plastic six-pack rings into the gutter grates. Little rocks suckle at the dirty water line. Pebbles caught under the rivulets reflect and spread, mysterious pried-open oysters rippling and beautiful.

It feels like someone else, someone much larger, has borrowed Mem's body and now she has to put it back on again, bone for bone. She is so tired she just wants to lie down in the turd-brown handfuls of cold mud and get colder and wetter and melt away, too. Mem is so tired she can't even breathe, can't remember how to make her lungs work. She just wants to go home but she doesn't even know what that means anymore, she is already home.

She hates that she is so upset for no reason. She is not a refugee in an occupied country, forced to walk days to the nearest border. She is not a three-hundred-pound woman who was electrocuted by her father. She was never "Trapped!" in a cabin during an avalanche, forced to cut off her own frostbitten toes in order to survive. She didn't have to walk in a death march. No one ever pushed her head into the toilet, flushing three times.

She remembers a show she saw on Aunt Raziel's TV, a science program about how the sound of snow falling is deafening to fish. When a snowflake lands in water, microscopic air bubbles trapped in its crystals squeak as they pop. The squeaking is as loud to the fish as a jackhammer would be for a human. All day when it snows, as people happily romp, the poor fish are bombarded with blaring squeals and screeches.

This is how Mem feels. No matter where she goes, no matter how quiet it seems to the rest of the world, inside her head it is deafening. She is bombarded by the noise of her own thoughts.

Earlier that morning, before Mem's mother left to go food shopping, she had made breakfast. She didn't really cook anything, she just poured milk into an open miniature box of brown cereal covered in sugar, the kind that Mem was never allowed to eat before her mother stopped working. Her mother didn't open a box for herself. She busied herself with tidying up the kitchen and hummed, a crisp white apron smoothed over her most expensive doole. She has taken to wearing her blacks day and night.

Mem understands. For a Wailer, the color black is not death, not black as blood or even black-and-blue-bruise-on-the-body black. It is not an absence of color. Black is loud, all of the colors playing at once and obliterating themselves out, an orchestra of sound so loud that nothing can be heard.

In Mem's house, instead of noise, there is a quiet that fills up all the empty space in the rooms, spreading the way smoke spreads, and shooing the ghosts away like flies. Watching her mother, Mem learns that loving someone means that you will inevitably grieve for them, that love is an engraved invitation for grief. But for grief there is no language, which makes no sense to Mem, since grief, like love, never really goes away. Life is just one long day separated into sections by sleep. Life never stops happening until you are dead. So whatever happens—love, grief, hate, shame—

never disappears. It just gets easier to live with. It just scabs over, waiting for something else significant to happen. And when that something else happens—another death, another love, another shameful episode—the scabs drop off and there are the original wounds, septic and drippy as ever.

Of course, it gets worse when there are more wounds, or when the original wound goes deeper, when it becomes a *puncture wound*. Mem imagines herself full of puncture wounds, deep as her whole self, starting at the skin where the welts blossom like flowering mold on the surface of bread. People usually just scrape mold off the top and eat the bread anyway, but Mem knows from the science shows she has watched that mold has invisible roots, flourishing their translucent threads through the body of the bread, unsuspected and unseen.

Mem knows you can get used to anything. Even the welts. Even the taste of see-through mold. Even the color black.

The color black is being alone. The color black is the fear of being alone, the cold flat fact that you will be alone for all of your life, even when you are around other people. Mem looks up at the black melting trees that line the street, gnarled fingers clutching at nothing. One tree has managed to split its whole upper self in two, growing into a semicircle of branches around power lines that run straight through the center. Both halves are fused together at the trunk, the part of the tree that grew as one thing before it was tall as the wires, then cleaved as if the wires were poisonous, as if the high voltage might kill it. As if it is just safer to disconnect.

What a shame to waste those tears, crying them for free, the ancestors would say to Mem, if they could see her then.

But Mem, sobbing, knows better.

Someone is always paying for tears.

— 1999 A.D., NEW YORK, UNITED STATES —

Excerpt from *Aurora's Pose*, essay by J. Mitchell

But why would a mother allow this to happen?

Maybe she didn't know. Maybe she didn't know any better. Maybe it was all she knew.

I have had a little while to think about this and what I've come to see is that this part of a Wailer's story is an old tale which can be found in its many versions across the world but always with the same players: a daughter, her mother, a wolf. In all of its incantations, the story still begs the question *why would a mother allow this to happen?* The quick answer is that the mother didn't know. But no matter how stupid, no well-meaning mother tarts her daughter up in bright red fabric and a basket of bait and then sends her off into the woods. No matter how stupid, any mother who knows enough to warn her daughter about the wolf knows what end awaits if the girl is sent off alone. The mother's warning is clearly false; she knows what's going to happen, in fact she's known all along. It happened to her, too. It's a village tradition that must be endured.

So why doesn't the mother just tell her the truth? Forget the red dress and edible lures, explain the situation and send her out. "It's your duty, don't be afraid. We all have to do it. It will be over before you know." It wouldn't work. The daughter would be scared; she would refuse to go. It's better like this, a set-up that cannot fail, a sweet and ignorant daughter who blunders into a situation she doesn't even realize should be frightening. Perhaps this way she won't figure out what's going on. Perhaps she might enjoy it.

But for a moment let's consider that the daughter isn't daft. Let's say she already knows, she's heard the stories. Being a girl, the daughter has already had to practice at being slower than she is, pretending things are okay when they're not. She doesn't mind it, because all she wants is to make her mother happy. If this means she must feign ignorance about the wolf—even behaving as if she were truly excited about the trip into the woods—then she will do it.

Like the daughter, we want to believe that in response to this show of loyalty the mother will be sad and regretful, not really wanting to send her daughter out but knowing she must. But this is not likely. Most probably she will be the kind of mother who's been so traumatized by her own experience with the wolf that she suffers nervous disorders and accidentally packs her daughter's basket with senseless things: a tin of meat without an opener, soap ends, a comb. The daughter is used to this and therefore lives in a constant state of mild exasperation. She will be equally aggravated once she's in the grandmother's house, going through the ridiculous motions of pretending that a wolf in bad drag is her grandmother. She will roll her eyes and tap her feet, sighing, arms crossed, waiting by the bed. Sometimes, if he's tired, the wolf lets this kind go, which is fine with the girl. Her mother won't know the difference anyway.

It seems the wolf prefers something more yielding, a daughter sent off by a mother who's pleased, as some fathers are pleased when their sons are sent off to war. This type of mother has incredible posture, she's steel-skinned and keenly conscious of all the ways in which the daughter will soon disappoint. The girl hasn't realized this yet and is therefore still trying, in every way, to please. The day of the trip into the woods, the mother wakes to find the daughter already dressed in her best riding cloak, having already baked the bread for the basket. The mother shakes her head. "Why would you wear your best cloak into the woods?" she asks. "It will get filthy and I'll be stuck washing it. Why haven't you let the bread cool? Your braids are a mess. You forgot the milk. There are ashes all over the floor. For the life of me I cannot comprehend why you will not stand up straight."

Like this mother, there are many mothers in the village who are grossly underrepresented in the story: lethargic or sad mothers who are too beleaguered to pack the basket, drunk mothers who sloppily cry and hug their daughters too hard and too long as they leave, widower fathers painfully aware of their own inadequacies as they crookedly plait the braids, mothers who are hardly ever home because of drink, drugs, love, lust, or business, their daughters waiting on the front porch, holding their baskets and chanting *she hasn't forgotten*. The daughter who has been left for good never gets to go into the woods, she's too busy caring for her incessantly hungry or dirty siblings. As she ages she'll develop elaborate fantasies about the wolf she never met, she'll dream of him while she washes the pissy linens for the millionth time, she will resent her young sisters as they go into the woods. She will never want children of her own.

But now I've skipped the point, which is this: No matter what sort of mother she has, once the red-hooded girl has entered the woods she will slow her pace and then stop. She will look down at the cobbled path and close her eyes, she will wish what every such girl from the dawn of history who has stood in this spot has wished: for her mother to run into the woods, weeping or laughing or calling, *I'm sorry*. For her mother to sweep her up into her arms. For her mother to stop this and just take her home.

Eventually, standing stock-still in the middle of the woods, the girl will realize that this is never going to happen. Hinging on this moment is a psychological destiny, a split second of unseen response that will determine whether this girl will grow to be strong or weak, sad or angry, afraid to leave the house or wired with a yearning for escape. Unlike her grandmother's house, which has two windows and a door, this is a moment from which there is no escape. The girl must see this, then she must carry on. She must pick up her foot and make it march over the mushrooms and moss. She must move steadily in the direction of her grandmother's house. She must go on, she must go without stopping, she must do this knowing full well that her grandmother is dead, the wolf is waiting, her mother is not coming to save her.

20

"How does a Wailer get out of the business?"

The air moves around rows of wet, shimmering melons with transparent skins shivering like giant peeled grapes in the middle of a field. Next to the melons are huge husks bundled together like corn, shoots steeping in inky pools trimmed with sunlight. From where Mem is standing, she can watch the husks unstick themselves from each other and shake off the leaves. There are bright yellow puppies inside, frantically rolling around on the marshy field, bumping into crates full of just-plucked melons. The melons split open and inside the pods are small babies, sunblind and covered in slime.

One of the babies doesn't look right. It is scrawny and gray, squirming in its slime pod without anyone to tend to it. It doesn't cry. Mem wants to go to it and pull it out of the muck but she can't, there are too many puppies in the way, wriggling like fat yellow worms. She would have to step on some of the puppies to save the baby, which is drowning inside of its own syrup.

It's not done yet, she says, and when she turns around she finds that she is on stage in the gallery, topless. She has only one breast but it is so exquisite that someone has framed it and there is a line of people waiting, tickets in hand, to see it. Mem doesn't mind. She thinks the breast is so lovely it should be looked at. Her mother is sitting in the corner of the gallery, looking forlorn and abandoned. She takes a drag from someone else's cigarette and says *that's not really her tit anyway* and when Mem looks down she sees that yes, the breast has been sewn on with thick and crooked black stitches. *Maybe you can sell it at the flea market,* her mother says, touching both sides of the breast and examining it.

But I like it, Mem says. Her mother laughs and the other people in the gallery laugh along with her. *It doesn't matter if you like it, it's only business,* her mother says. *And it's not even yours. Try to be more professional.* She begins to unbutton her own shirt. *Here,* she says, *let me show you how.*

Mem's last funeral takes place in a cemetery which is located on the far corner of a busy intersection. There used to be lovely tall trees surrounding the graveyard, closing it off so no one driving by could see in, but the year before a woman trying to make a left turn slammed into another driver's car. Both drivers claimed that the cemetery trees had blocked their view, so the district council decided the trees had to go. Now the cemetery is surrounded by stumps and gas stations and parked cars and exhaust fumes and a U-Store-It complex full of mausoleums for people's things. Without the trees, Mem feels as naked as the cemetery.

I am a professional, she tells herself as she stands behind the mourners, mostly men in business suits with impenetrable masks for faces and their dry mouths pinched closed. The client had requested that Mem wear anything but black and wait to perform until after the visiting mourners had gone. Mem said that would be fine; she has been honoring more and more of these requests from people who admire her work but are afraid of legal action.

The surviving daughter had called Mem the week before, begging her to come. "Please," said the woman, her voice on the verge of cracking. "I didn't know my father very well but it was in the will to hire you. He was a very prominent man, a politician. It was his last wish."

Mem waits for the mourners to get into their cars. She begins to cry, chokes it back, watching the backs of the unprofessionals. She envies them their public lives. She envies that when they go home they will be able to take off their black suits and dresses, that, eventually, they will be allowed to stop mourning. This all makes Mem cry harder. She cries so hard she feels rigid around her own edges, body-shaped tourniquet crushing her, squeezing tighter with each sob. Mem cries so hard her whole self comes out of her mouth and eyes, another self coming out, the little ghost-Mem, condensed and hardened, bullet-shaped, squatting and cursing inside of Mem's head. Something inside of Mem bubbles, the bubbles break, she waits for the color to come up but it isn't a color at all. This time it is a sound, a hot leaking like air escaping from a tire. Mem clamps her hand over her mouth to stop it, but she knows it will find its way out anyway.

The woman who hired Mem comes closer. She is thin, blond, about fifty years old. She quickly whispers something over her shoulder to a teenage boy who had been tapping his shoes, twisting his suit buttons, and flicking the hair out of his eyes since the service began. Mem has seen this behavior before and knows from her mother that sometimes boys have the hardest time at the burials of their fathers and grandfathers. There is always something they never got to say. Or something they needed to hear that was never said by someone else. Rough claps-on-the-back instead of *I love you*. Handshakes instead of hugs.

The boy lopes over to one of the cemetery's sparse remaining trees and slouches next to it. There is a sudden light wind and the tree, still leafless but covered in a thousand green seed casings, drops a crackling storm of green helixes onto the boy.

Dabbing at her own swollen eyes, the woman walks over to Mem. The woman says, in a clear, strong voice, "Thank you, thank you so much, Mirabelle. You were very moving. You certainly have earned your reputation. I'd like to pay you now, if that's okay. I must admit I'm somewhat relieved that it's all over."

Mem lowers her head in gratitude.

It will never be over, thinks Mem. *No matter how much you pay, you will be losing him over and over and over again for the rest of your life. Every birthday. Every holiday. Your shellac won't last long. It will wash right off.*

The woman's hands shake only a little as they fumble through a brown briefcase for the fee. She pulls out a thick envelope and hands it to

Mem. The name *Mirabelle* is written across the top, spiky and uneven, the shape of a soap-opera heart attack on a hospital monitor. The moment the envelope touches Mem's fingers she sees something in the shape of the woman's carefully painted mauve mouth that reminds her of a character in a dream.

"I have something else for you, something I promised my father I would give to you if you came," says the woman, pulling an overstuffed manila envelope out of her bag. "You know, he considered himself an expert on your people."

Mem accepts the heavy envelope but has no idea what to say. She stares at the mouth. "Well," says the mouth, "I have company expecting me. Thank you again." She smiles uncomfortably and walks toward the parking lot where the twitchy young man is waiting.

Mem examines the envelope. It has a computer-printed label on the front that says *Rep. Anthony J. DePaul, Jr.*

Mem knows this name. DePaul. She hears her mother's voice in her mind, *Fuck DePaul.* Now she remembers; DePaul is the man who started the Wailing Prohibition. He's the one who's been shutting them all down. Mem peels the sticky flap of the envelope back and pulls out a pile of not very pristine paper. Some of the pages have been typed with an old-fashioned typewriter, some are covered in different kinds of handwriting, and there are several sheets of photocopied pages from books, as well as pages of poetry, excerpts from research papers, newspaper articles, and penciled research notes, all about Wailers. Mem opens the pay envelope. The inside is full of so many bills that they are compressed together into bundles bound by strips of paper from the bank. When Mem pulls the bills out she sees that the one on top is a thousand-dollar bill, and when she flips through the stacks they are all the same as the one on top. She counts two hundred of them. And then she knows.

She has just mourned for the old man, the man with the meaty fingers, the man whose ghostness has haunted her for so long.

And now she can leave her mother.

— 1934 A.D., BUENOS AIRES, ARGENTINA —

Found in a love letter to Zenouthia, a local Weeping Maid
notorious for having many suitors of both sexes

I want

         to tease the pulp out of you
with my small hands stretching
over your octaves,

         to remember
that a symphony of lips and
tongues and hands
can smooth me
into a thousand poppies
turning at once
towards the sun,

         to know your moss and get
dirt between my teeth,

         to never again
take cruel leave of my body,
the splitting figs, the absinthe strokes
from the deceiving arms of Shiva,
every palm musk and creaming
over with the first press
of little deaths,

     oh so that this will never
     be the memory of a memory,
     a waterwashed gravestone,
     hand-me-down shadow, no
I want

         my lips gasping
at the root of it now,

press me down now
like a warm wax stamp
on this moment, this
instant, don't
let me forget.

21

"Where is your mother now?"

The walk home from the old man's funeral is so dreamy that Mem forgets about her body altogether. Balloons, balloons, this is what she is made of, the world is made of, the air is soft as bathwater. In her hands she carries the magic thing she had always known would come, a magic key to save her. Her steps gently rock her inside body in waves. There will be no more business, no more wailing, no more searching for something that cannot be found. She has found it, it has found her, it is in her hands and she is only steps away from delivering herself into a new life.

Standing still and silent for a moment in front of the screen door, Mem lets her breath catch up with her. There are thin cobwebs across the top of the shrubs under the window. The air smells of fabric softener from all of the drier vents blowing from the houses. She wants to wait to find out what happens next. She understands that this is it, one of those moments before the moment when everything changes. Usually one is not as aware, such moments being for most people rare and unpredictable. But Mem's life has groomed her to accept this unpredictability, to expect it. In fact, it is perhaps the only consistent thing she has ever known. For once she welcomes it. She cannot wait.

In spite of this, Mem is totally unprepared when Sofie opens the storm door from the inside, convulsively sobbing, and says through the screen that Mem's mother is dead.

In a hysterical rush, Sofie tells Mem that her mother died while visiting one of the Aunts. She put down her coffee cup, collapsed onto the floor, and never got back up again. All-of-a-sudden, although Mem knows that there is no such thing. Had Aunt Ayin been there, breasts hovering over her mother like impending doom? With Aunt Ayin attached to the breasts, sweating, her hair sticking out like a child's drawing of sun beams? Weeping genuinely as she lit candles and applied balms, knowing that it was too late?

No, says Sofie, no one was there but one of the old Aunts neither of them knows. "My mother sent me here to tell you," she says. She is here to tell Mem. Her mother is dead.

"But there's more," Sofie wails. "Someone called the police to report us and now they're coming here! They're coming to all our houses! My mother doesn't know what to do."

Mem doesn't know what to do. She is confused. "Didn't you call an ambulance?" she asks. "Maybe you're wrong. Maybe she's just sick. Why are the police coming?"

"No! She's dead!" Sofie screams. Her face is mottled pink, red, white, the colors of a tight fist. "She's dead and now the police are coming! My mother said to find all of the evidence and get rid of it! My mother said to get rid of it!" Mem is suddenly very light again, her joints pleasantly disconnected in a weightless space. She rests a hand softly on top of her cousin's hysterically jerking shoulder. The hair at the crown of Sofie's head is wet. She smells like the inside of a deli.

"You better get a hold of yourself before they get here. Go into the kitchen and wait," says Mem. She can almost see the shape of the words drifting out of her mouth and into the air. They come out like buds, they flower and float. She pats Sofie's moist shoulder. "You have to let it go now. It's better this way.

"Everything will be okay."

In the basement, where she was never allowed to go, this is what Mem finds:

- a ten-pound bag of large-crystal salt from the *Via Salaria*
- dozens of small silver-plated lockets and snuff boxes
- a paper shredder
- a leaf-bag full of shredded paper
- a small silver key hung on a finishing nail near the door

None of these things seem like evidence. Behind the paper shredder, Mem discovers two baby food jars full of small teeth with long, pronged roots. It takes her a moment to realize that these are her teeth, her baby teeth, collected and kept from so many years ago. Mem picks up one of the jars and the teeth tinkle against each other like shells.

The dust itches her nose and inside of her ears, she can feel the little key getting hot in her palm. She looks through the stark basement, hunting for the thing which can be unlocked by the key. Under the table, there is something square-shaped tethered to the underside of the table with masking tape. Mem works the tape edges with her left hand, prying off as much of it as she can until she feels the thing give way.

It is an antique salt cellar on its side, a redwood box with a hinged lid and a small lock, the kind they used in France during the three hundred years of the *gabelle* tax. A place to store the most precious of commodities. *Countless wars were fought for salt. So many people died. They died in battle. They died in the mines. They lived in cities built in blocks of salt underground but they were not safe there, even though salt houses don't burn.* Whole generations were born underground and then died in the salt digging galleries. At Aunt Ayin's house years ago Mem had seen pictures of these underground cities, with chapels, houses, center squares, and stables carved out of salt, looking almost like the Moon Mansion she once dreamed of, a sheltered cave of pure whiteness of the salt garden, a true salt cellar, a city of salt.

The salt box is about ten inches deep, narrow and heavy, but Mem can tell it is not filled with salt. She sits on the floor, puts the box on her lap and fits the key into the lock. It slips in and turns without any resistance. The lid creaks when Mem lifts it.

Inside the box, at the top, is Mem's mother's dimpled locket on a chain, resting on part of an old greeting card decorated with flowers and trees.

Mem puts the locket aside and pulls the card out to reveal a stack of paper money, hundreds of bills all going in one direction, enough to be every fee Mem has ever collected. There are scores of wrinkled twenties, thumbed-over fifties, crisp one-hundred-dollar bills as thick as the box is deep. On the other side of the greeting card Mem's mother has written, *For Mem, so you will never have to weep again.*

Mem turns the card over, examines the jaunty lilies and daisies that thrive in the picture. She strokes the flowers.

Something bright red shoots through the short block-glass window at the top of the stairway wall and whips across the basement. This is immediately followed by an identical thing but this time blue. Then red again. Then blue. Mem realizes she is holding the salt cellar so tightly against her chest that the corners are digging pink grooves into her forearms. The police lights enter and sweep, enter and sweep.

Mem thinks, this could be Rome, four thousand years ago, those lights could be torches, this could be Fiji as the men came to civilize us all to death, or the gallows in England, or a witch-hunt, a chase. There is a knocking at the front door. Breathing steadily, Mem slides the box under a tool table and makes her way up the stairs.

— 1710 A.D., Bruton, England —

<small>PAMPHLET INSERT</small>
Author Unknown

Caveat
In Defense of the Prohibition of Weeping Maids

The Matter has been solemnly debated, and we insist on a Proper show of Justice in the matter. Traces of this Decrepit Cult, so valued by the most vulgar of minds, are still to be found conducting their Savage Orgies as their stock-in-trade; all Virtuous folk should reserve their mourning to their own homes.

22

"Why won't you just tell us your name?"

The police are at the door. Mem sees one of them through the foyer window. He has burnt-orange hair and a thin-lipped mouth. Sofie is whimpering. "Don't open it!" But Mem does, and the sound of voices and radios blur together into a puddle of meaninglessness, like something exotic. Mem looks at the policeman, his ruddy hue, his thin lips. He looks familiar and not-familiar, out-of-focus. Mem looks again and his face wavers like a reflection on water, shrinking smaller and tight till she sees it, finally. The face of the boy who had pissed his pants when they buried his father, one of her earliest funerals.

There are the same green eyes. The same furtive blink.

There is the same carrot-colored hair.

Mem remembers the face, the hair, the tears that had bathed his face till it shined while patches of urine bloomed through the crotch of his shorts. At the time, the girls had been pretty impressed. They had pointed and whispered about the boy sobbing and peeing and cowering behind his mother's black-stockinged legs and they wished with all their might that they, too, could be so moved. Mem had watched the boy cry with such envy, thumbing her doole's bell-shaped layers and small blue flowers. Behind them she could hear her own mother sob, wailing, the burst tearing of hems. Young Derasha, still healthy and rude. The mothers wept almost in unison, like the rounds of a folk lyric. Like a duet.

She lets the man in. He returns Mem's stare and asks, "Are you Mirabelle?"

Sofie has run into the kitchen. Mem follows her, sees her sitting on one of the kitchen chairs, her body rocking back and forth. This is real rocking, the kind that madness brings as you try to find balance again. A chaotic soul set on a rocking chair. Sofie is loose and watery, without her mother to tell her what is happening and thicken her soul like stew.

"What are you going to tell them?" Sofie whispers before the man follows Mem in.

"I don't know," Mem whispers back. "Maybe the truth."

"Which truth?" Sofie asks.

"What do you mean, which truth?" says Mem. "How many can there be?"

Mem watches the redheaded policeman's beetle-shiny shoes pace from one end of the plank-patterned linoleum floor to the other. The policeman has been following Mem's work for years. His questions do not surprise her, they are the same ones she has been asked by strangers since she was six years old.

"Is it true you worship goddesses and never went to school?"

"Is it true your mothers torture you to teach you how to cry?"

"Do you know it's against the law?"

"Have you ever lived in hiding?"

"Where is your mother now?"

As always, Mem doesn't answer but she is very polite. She listens to his questions and stares at the little mounds her knees make under the black cloth. Her kneecaps start to ache from sitting in the same position for so long because her mother's kitchen chairs are made for a much taller person, a normal-sized person whose heels reach the ground when they sit. The redheaded policeman is tall enough to comfortably sit in a chair, but he doesn't sit. He stands stiffly, hands awkwardly clasped on his belt. He stares, as if he is expecting Mem to burst into tears, or song, or tell him a long and eloquent story.

Of course, she could do this. She could tell stories.

But the policeman doesn't want stories, he wants secrets. He wants her name.

Mem thinks, *What is the difference between a secret and a lie? A secret is a lie you tell yourself.* Now Mem thinks that secrets are really just lies waiting to be searched for and found, that every secret is shielded by and conjoined to a succulent, flowering lie, so the true story is always made up of what has been hidden, and what has been left behind. Mem tries to not look at the policeman's mouth, at the five long red hairs growing from the tip of his nose, but his smile looks so artificial, sewn into place the way a corpse's lip-drift is repaired by mending the mouth with thread, like a cushion, from inside and then pinned through a nostril. He says, *You girls are the real victims here. We only want to help you,* and his lips are so thin they are almost not there. She watches those lips ask her for her secret name so many times that the name seems more important than the real reason why the police are there, as if not telling him her name is the true crime.

A few times Mem catches a different expression on the policeman's face, a quick look of sheer disbelief. He must be wondering how it is possible that this scared and scrawny child is the famous young woman they've been hunting for so long. He glances down at Mem's face, her hands, her posture, her dress, trying to figure out how she does it, as if she is rigged with tubes, like a weeping statue of Mary. The look on his face says, *This can't be the one.*

Still he hopes. This is probably the case that could make his career, the first successful interrogation of an infamous Wailer, and in her own home. This is why he's being kind, but not too kind, hoping to carefully push her into defending her mother or her history. He cannot wait for her to start talking so that he can tilt his head to the side and nod while he writes. He will look very concerned.

When the policeman checks his watch for a second, the soles of his shoes crunching against the salt on the floor, Mem looks at Sofie who mouths the words, *DON'T TELL.* She is rocking back and forth, worrying her own black lace hem as if she is polishing her fingertips, which are usually peeled down and raw from the biting that is her habit when she weeps. At that moment, amazingly, she is not weeping, and her eyes are the color blue before blue disappears, almost no-color, rimmed with red and hard water. Exposed like skinned and parboiled fruit.

No don't cover your face, you have to feel exposed! Mem remembers when she saw her first news show on Aunt Raziel's TV and learned about a group of homeless men who had died of exposure. Mem didn't understand that *exposure* had to do with the cold weather, the slow losing of your self through fingertips and toes. It had just made sense to her that someone could die from feeling exposed. Or from being exposed by someone else. Overexposed, like a negative in too-bright light.

There is no bright light in Mem's mother's kitchen. Out of the kitchen window, between the sweeping red flash of the police lights, the half-moon has begun to secrete a vaguely radiant hoop. Mem thinks about Aunt Ayin's story about the moon, but she remembers the part of the story everybody forgets to tell, how the moon's loss wasn't caused by things taken away or denied. The moon did this all to herself, because she would not listen. She had first been loved, then warned, then shut off and left behind. Now the moon is ashamed of her early bravado, her childish conceit, because this is what she really was underneath that loud pageantry after all—an overcast planet of scars and bone. An old mothball no longer useful. An embarrassed hung head. A disreputable daughter.

In the midst of the strange fog of unreality that has settled about her, Mem hears, *It's better this way. You have to let go. So sorry for your loss.* Mem has heard these words a thousand times, a litany of useless things the mourners say, but she knows now that none of them work. Those ideas are based on untruths and fear, a culture that puts stock in sudden emotional catharsis. When they pay her to perform they are hoping that somehow there will be a deliverance through tears, a passageway through which things will be better, they will learn to let go, whatever is lost will be found. They never expect to be stuck in a place where the things or people they love are never coming back.

"When is your mother coming back?" asks the policeman.

What Mem really wants to see is what the policeman looks like now when he cries. Mem wonders how long it would take to make it happen, how much of her sad story he would viciously scribble onto his pad before he decides that it is unbearable to go on. How long it would take to make him fall apart, for Mem to find the fissure, wiggle it open, drop in some salt. Mem thinks she should use a stopwatch. She should take bets. First she would bet that he doesn't even know what he looks like when he is crying. Like all of the unprofessionals, Mem thinks, he probably doesn't want to know. All they ever seem to want to know is how to make it stop.

Mem, jiggling her legs under the table, is the only one left who knows how to make it stop. If she answers his questions it will stop the whole thing, all six thousand years of it, right here, forever. No one will realize this until it is too late, until the articles and exposés and books are out, and people are holding her story in their hands. Like the policeman, the readers will say, *tell me*. They will ask the same questions that have been asked for thousands of years. They will be so moved they will read it twice. *Tell me again*. Where would Mem begin?

The policeman cocks his head to the side like the mourners do when they talk to widows, an approximation of what they think sympathy is supposed to look like. *It's not your fault*, he says. Cocked head, repetitive nod, knit brows. *We don't know how your kind even managed to survive.*

Mem looks at Sofie and is suddenly surprised to see how much she still looks like the little girl she used to be. There is the same plain brown hair. The same small feet. The same old lady's chin poking through a soft big-ness-waiting-to-get-out. As if you could cut her in half lengthwise with a butter knife and it would sink right through, hitting no bones. Sofie looks wet. Worried. Like herself, only more so. How old is she? How young? Mem looks at Sofie and knows that all her ages are still there, solidified in layers like the colors of a jawbreaker.

The policeman rubs his thumbs against the bones above his eyes and finally sits down, sighing. He says, *You know we'll find your names by morning*, but Mem looks past the kitchen window with its strawberry-patch curtains and cannot even imagine the morning. The hard blue light pulls tendons across the sky and spreads inky fingers over the house. The sky was still bright when the policemen had emerged from the edges of Mem's court that day, driving their wagons right up onto the grass.

If Aunt Ayin were there in the kitchen she would say, *Cross those legs Sofie this instant before a ghost flies up in between them!* But Aunt Ayin is probably out alerting the rest of the Aunts, sweating and shaking her two chins and adjusting her too-tight doole. Aunt Ayin is probably sobbing, out-of-key, cracking the hems of her blacks with her hips. Syrupy makeup dripping down her face in sticky slow motion as her bulbous heft rises and falls. *Overdone. Unprofessional*, Mem's mother would have muttered. *What would the ancestors say?*

Of course, they would have said, "Don't tell."

Mem thinks about telling the policeman that her name is Aurora, but he will not get the joke.

The policeman scratches the underside of his chin, which is bearded with dozens of little pink pimples. He, too, gazes stupidly out of the little window. In a moment, the policeman is going to turn toward Mem, lean closer, and ask her for the secrets. In a moment, for the hundredth time that night, he is going to rub the bones above his eyes and ask Mem for her name.

And for the millionth time in her life she will not know what to say.

— 1564 A.D., PAKISTAN —

Hindi Poem from a Master Wailer to her daughter

my daughter I have cursed you
to a life of broken bracelets.
though the world will one day pay to drink
the honey of your cries
your hands
will always bear ashes
and you will never dance anywhere.

23

"Do you bury your dead in the same cemeteries where you work?"

In the cemetery, it is dark and Mem's doole blends into the darkness around her. From where she is standing, about two hundred yards away from the tent, she can just make out the candles and the flowers and the white blur of faces, the only things illuminated in the darkness. Some of the Aunts have arrived early, already weeping, staggering like drunks as they walk to the site. Mem watches as Hector distributes the red velvet pouches full of fees, calmly weaving through the parade of blacks, as if all the screaming and snotting and breast-beating were the most natural thing in the world. Behind the tent, the horizon line disappears between the deep blue of the night sky and the deep gray of the burial hills, all of it so close to black that it is almost impossible to tell where one ends and the other begins.

In the half-light, Mem's bare arms look blue, although Mem knows now that even the idea of the blue is a trick. A program on Aunt Raziel's television once taught her that our eyes only see reflections of light that are shot from object to eye to brain like a pinball. So maybe, Mem thinks, the color blue people see is just an illusion, the brain's idea of blue. Maybe the true color of blue, if we could see it without our eyes, is a brilliant pink, brighter than our own eyes can articulate. Maybe any one color blue contains within it a thousand shades that blend and flash like the kaleidoscope wings of a dragonfly. Perhaps the color blue that she sees depends on everything else around it: the temperature, the lighting, the age she is when she sees it, the music playing in the background, the color blue someone else tells her it is. Maybe, no matter how sophisticated we think the mechanism of our eyes might be, when it comes to the colors—like everything else—something is forever lost in translation.

From where Mem is standing, she can hear the Aunts already trying to outdo each other as they huddle by the flowers around her mother's fresh grave. Across the field she hears fabric ripping, unfamiliar shrieks. Mem has never been to a circus but this is what she always imagined it would look like, clowns and performers standing around in a circle, under a tent, putting on a show.

Her mother's voice plays in her ear. *In all that you do, you must honor your ancestors. Remember the privilege, the celebrity, the sacred distinction. Our black silks. The gold coins. Our shimmering tear-colored jewels. Remember the way the firelight made our tears shine when the torch-bearers bowed down as we passed, afraid to whisper or even breathe. With every breath of your own you should remember them, remember this, relive the grandeur and the glory no matter the era in which you live.*

It had taken over four hours to call them all but Mem had taken her time. She went through her mother's list and called each one personally. She said *no veils or onion or soap, just blacks and handkerchiefs,* and none was able to refuse. It was an irresistible offer, the glory of their ancestry finally come to life again in a decadent orgy of crying. A million small deaths. A dark harvesting.

Mem wrote down the names of all of those who had confirmed that they would come and the dollar amount they agreed to be paid. When she finished licking the last fee envelope closed, when there was no money left in the salt cellar or the old man's envelope, she put her mother's locket around her neck and called the redheaded policeman. She tapped the edge of the locket and waited. She was still floating. She still could not believe that the locket hadn't vanished in small puffs of smoke, that her mother's things would still exist while she did not.

Other than Aunt Ayin and Sofie, there are no other surviving relatives by the grave. There is no man of the cloth. Instead, the paid Wailers sway around the hole, shaking and muttering like the audience of a television evangelist, a mass of zealots speaking in tongues. Now Mem understands why the mourners in Fiji knock their own teeth out. Why they cut their fingers off. Why they blacken their bodies with charcoal or plaster themselves in white pipe clay, cutting their scalps with shells and bleeding into the graves. Mem would do any of this if it would prolong her not having to feel anything.

Mem saw the outside of the casket and the burial hole before she hid herself, before the others came. The hole, she knows now, is important. She sees that everything about death has to do with the hole. Mouth holes, grave holes, eye holes. Holes where, physically, the person used to be. *The walking wounded*. This is a term Mem's mother used to describe surviving loved ones who were not grieving well, the kind of people who you could just look at and see that they were full of holes, like the ghosts of shot soldiers, riddled with tubes of light. Now Mem is full of holes that cannot be filled. They are so big the word *hole* doesn't suit them. Now the holes are *cavities, craters, gorges, voids. Chasms. Pits.*

Mem fills her hands with her face.

In her mind Mem hears her mother, the rhythm and pitch of her mother's anguish as it used to sound behind her at the jobs. It was almost the sound of hysterical laughter, a ruined noise, the sound of things breaking. Hearing it makes Mem wish she could cry. The sound of the Wailers by the grave blends into a smooth all-pitch throb, like a soup whose individual spices have become indistinguishable. A deep-mouthed dragon's breath, a chorus of sighs.

They wail, for their money, for their lives. They wail as if it will be the last time.

Only Mem knows that it is.

For the last time. Mem already knows, she's known forever: everything we do, we do for the last time. The first time. The one-and-only time. The almost-lost time, shaped into uniqueness by everything else around it: the temperature, the lighting, the age you are when you do it. The music playing in the background. The act that someone else tells you it is.

And so for the first time, the last time, the one-and-only almost-lost time, Mem tries to wail, for her mother, for herself. She wants to be wailing, she wants true wailing, for it to sound like what it means, she wants to wail in the darkness so loud and so rich that she won't be able to hear the sirens as the paddy-wagons pull up onto the grass by the hole. But nothing comes out.

And then Mem says, out loud, to no one, "My name is Mem."

And then what happens?

Nothing happens.

The Earth does not open to suck her in. Mem's mother does not rise from the dead to scold her. Things keep on going. They keep on happening. Nothing happens and everything is still happening, no matter what Mem says or does or reveals, just as nothing happens and everything keeps happening no matter who has died. Mem was the secret. And now she is revealed, her papery layers undressed, blinking in the warm moonlight, even as it streams through the sky. She reaches out to touch the light and it splits over her fingers like warm wax so that for a moment, she forgets where she is, where she is going, even where she has been.

"Mem," she says.

It once came from a secret upside-down tree with roots reaching to the sky like a head of old fingers stirring up the cosmos like soup. Now it comes from her, from her mouth. She watches the policemen close in from all around the site, ushering the women into the wagons. Mem unwraps her hair from its tight bun, shaking it out with her fingers. The strands are bent into a bun-shape, sore, feeling as if they are going to snap right off her head when she moves them. There are small, waxy buttercups by Mem's feet and she understands about the flowers now, why people keep partnering them with dead or dying things. Mem knows there was a time when the flowers were necessary to cover the smell of rotted corpses, but she never understood why you would want to honor the dead with more dead things, garish plant genitals posed childishly, stupid whorls of dead color, healthless and stooped as the mourners who paid for them. Now she sees that it is very simple: *without corpses there would be no flowers*. It is the basis for all life on Earth, an exchange so fleeting our primitive eyes never get to see it. Small, small, small, we fall apart, we disperse, our parts reorganizing themselves to become something else. There is no such thing as unfinished business.

Beneath Mem's feet there is a purring in the grass, the sound of things eating, copulating, dying. It is almost as loud as the dark swarm of Japanese beetles that invaded the summer before, covering all of the new leaves with their metallic machinery. They were unlike any insect Mem had ever seen before, like shiny beads of mercury with wings or little flying clocks. People set caged traps in their backyards to catch them and all summer you could smell the lure. But the beetles settled on the leaves anyway and left delicate lattice patterns where green used to be, silvery filigree where sunlight seamed through, casting honey-bright patterns onto the ground, more delicate than humans could ever embroider. At the end of each day all of the neighbors had poured the cages full of beetles into trash bags or sacks. It was easy to tell they were still alive because they swarmed in currents under the plastic.

Above Mem's head the three-quarter moon broods. Her mother used to sweep a Q-tip dipped in peroxide under the pale half-moons of her nails to clean them and keep them white. She'd say, *It's the nails and hair that keep growing after you're buried*. Mem tries to imagine her mother's spectacular hair and strong nails growing at fast-forward speed, like those three-minute-long nature films of plants budding over weeks.

Tonight the moon is translucent as a fingernail, but Mem no longer believes the moon is shame-faced. She thinks that maybe the moon likes to be dull, glad for shadows and relieved to be left in her powdery bedclothes, a saucer of salt for nobody's wound. After all, it takes her a month just to get out of bed. Maybe she smokes when no one is looking. Maybe these stories, poems, and songs make her restless, she can't be bothered. She doesn't like riddles, she is not an enchantress folding delicately into her papery crags. She is nobody's halo or mistress or sister, and the stars are just crumbs in her sheets. Every night she sets her paltry light like a bored eye, she chants with each revolution, *It's not my fault.*

Mem shifts to better position herself to watch the last of the police cars pull away. She can smell the earthy scent of herself wafting up through the doole. Her own unstirred broth. It is the smell of a fisted salt bud breaking the soil. A seed pearl of salt plucked up from the muck. An unwashed salt truffle just sniffed out, dusty with restless loam and dew.

Mem, unpeeled and blinking in the moonlight.

Mem knows that this summer the beetles will not come with their machine-metal clicks and whirs, those voluptuous bags of humming jewelry that enter nightmares, under sacks of potatoes. The pristine green leaves will stay ripe. They will only crinkle a little, at the edges. Like parched tongues. Like water.

— 1897 A.D., AIX EN PROVENCE, FRANCE —

On Her Deathbed, Master Babbette to Her Daughter

How can you be sad
When this Now is leaking its good milk,
Your soul's syrup taps still drizzling cool
And melancholy sap?
How can you be sad when you
Are truly Muse and Goddess
And the Gatekeeper kicking up dust?
Oh my daughter, do not miss me,
I will wait faithfully at the pulsing mouth
Of Hades, rattling the gate
And coupling with demons.
I will visit the little boys in their sleep
And gloat at God with my mouth full of nectar.
So stop hording the peaches
Engorged with wise water. Eat
So that you too will be
Flushed with memory and someday old,
Hair peach-thinned and colorless
Your flesh soft and sage and tasting of ash.
Till then wear armor or ball gowns and dance
Till you buckle the floors with your feet.
Savage the linens, the silver,
The holiday meat,
The fat beasts, the bloodwine,
Do not forget your name.
Thrash at cobwebs
And burn the clutter,
Shatter the windows

And gluttonous doors
But think of me and throw red petals
About the room
As often as you can.

24

"But why would a mother do this to her own child?"

Across the city from where her own funeral is taking place, Celeste stands in the small foyer in Aunt Raziel's old apartment, holding her bags and facing the door.

Celeste is leaving. She is tired. It doesn't even make sense for her to be carrying any bags at all. Why pack and carry a lifetime around with you when you don't really have that long to go? But it's not the bags that are weighing her down, it's the room, the air, the light, her consciousness.

She tells herself, for the thousandth time, *It is the only way.*

This way her daughter will only have to mourn once, instead of the thousand times she'd mourn Celeste each moment they stayed together. Yes, for her daughter this will be a hard mourning, but it will only be once. And it will be the last.

Hector has taken care of everything. Hector of the calm and soothing voice and broken eyes, Hector who has been a little bit in love with Celeste since the first time he hired her more than two decades ago. He helped to choose the plot, the time, the perpetual care, the *schiva* platters, even the headstone, which, once unveiled, will simply say in Hebrew: *They are not long, the weeping and the laughter.*

As always there must be flowers. When Celeste was little there were such enormous blooms. Their wide-mouth stink invisibly rose and spread like the transparent fingers of steam that rise from pots about to boil. The

bright petals annoyed her even then, no matter how lovely. Her first dresses were trimmed in flowers, too, small and blue but she didn't mind
because they spun into blurs when she twirled.

Celeste puts the fingertips of her right hand around the hollow brass
doorknob and at first the touch is so cold her fingers jerk back a little in
surprise. She relaxes her fingers but they still just rest there, they will not
turn. She cannot open the door. Why doesn't she open the door?

It dawns on her that this moment has already occurred. She doesn't
believe it is possible to relive any part of one's life but she remembers this,
her right hand barely touching the doorknob, her left hand squeezed
around the money he had given her, she had just closed the door, she was
shaking. What had he said? *If you don't let me hire her I will turn you in.* He
said, *They'll take her away and send you to jail.* Neither of these had made
her flinch. Who did he think he was, this decrepit old letch? Didn't he
know who he was talking to? If he was willing to spend so much money,
Celeste had thought, if he had the balls to threaten her here, in her own
house, he would be easy to manipulate. She thought she could play on his
sense of power, she could milk this fucker dry. And then he said, *This is
your last chance. You will never see your daughter again.*

Why didn't she open the door?

Celeste without her daughter.

She remembers the day of Mem's naming, before any of the Aunts
came to celebrate, how she had scattered handfuls of sacred salt from the
Via Salaria across her patchy new lawn and watched as the rain pulled it
down into the soil. Ayin said the rain was a good sign and read, aloud,
what her books had to say about things Saturnine, Aquarius: *of water,
sour, tart and dead, opium and those things which stupefy, and those which are
never sown, and never bear fruit, or only bring forth black fruit, as the Cypress
tree used at burials, as the herb pas-flower which they strew in graves before the
bodies, and creeping things, solitary, sad and nightly, fearful, melancholy, and
those that eat their young.* When Ayin noticed that Celeste was ignoring her,
she had closed the book and put out the bowls of potato salad and maca-

roni salad and tuna salad and several bags of rolls, sweating and panting the whole time, feeling her sister ungrateful for all the effort.

"Why do you keep your bread on top of the refrigerator instead of inside it?" she clucked as she passed with her arms full of soda bottles, rushing so that she could pick up Sofie, who had begun to cry again. "Don't you know it could get moldy?"

Mem, born exactly two days and three months later than Sofie, was in the bassinet next to Sofie, and she was not crying. In fact, she had never cried, not even at the moment of birth. She seemed nonplussed by the wet, loud, cold world around her and simply moved her arms through the new clear space as Aunt Ayin rocked Sofie with one arm and lit more candles with the other. The flames of the candles licked at the reflection of water drizzling down the wall opposite the bassinets.

"Get me a clean vial," said Celeste to Ayin. "A small one."

Ayin fiddled through drawers, the stretched seams of her dress groaning, punctuating her labored breathing, the fumbling noises and torrents outside. *Dry cleaners shrunk it again.* Celeste looked at the quiet creature in her cradle and her own eyes filled with tears. Ayin made a triumphant little wheezing noise when she found the vial and handed the glass tube to Celeste, who lifted Mem out of the cradle. "Watch her head!" Ayin cried out unnecessarily.

Celeste admired Mem's toes, lined up like baby sweet peas on a knife. She flicked the bottom of Mem's foot with her fingernail, but Mem barely stirred.

Celeste flicked harder, then pinched Mem's ankle, and the baby shifted, just a little, in her blanket. The rain got louder, then quiet, then loud again, as if it couldn't make up its mind. Celeste, who was not an anxious woman, began to get anxious. She pulled at a piece of flesh on Mem's upper arm where it folded over the elbow like a freshly-baked roll.

She pinched it and was surprised at how soft it was, how it gave way between her broad fingers like clay. Still Mem did not cry. She seemed, instead, fascinated by the world around her, thrilling with the movement of her tiny arms flailing between dust motes and the shadows of raindrops cast on the blanket.

Celeste pinched harder.

And harder.

And harder, until finally, Mem's face became closed and red as an apple, Mem's whole self closing and then opening with a silent choking first, then a wail, and then sobs, her lungs filling with new air.

Celeste slid the vial along Mem's cheek, meticulous to catch each hot drop. She handed the vial to Aunt Ayin, who closed it up with a wax stopper and looked a little disappointed; Sofie's wails had never been that loud.

"Oh, Mem, that's good, that's right," said Celeste, holding Mem to her breast, rocking her back to a safe place, back to quiet, where Mem's sobs melted into soft hiccups.

Later Celeste would boil these tears with sacred salt, let the crystals climb up the string and scrape them into a locket. It was bad luck to wear your children's tears, the worst luck of all. Celeste knew this. But she would do it anyway. *Let it be my own bad luck*, she thought, *and not my daughter's. Let me carry her tears with me wherever I go.*

When she looked at her daughter, the love that came over her was without warning and immense, opening its many arms like flowers, filling up the room and bursting through the glass of the windows, its vines and fruits as warm and thick as blood and older than Celeste would ever be. She was a strong woman but she knew she would never be strong enough for this love that now filled and overfilled her like an ocean unfurling its waves into a thimble. Where did it come from? How would she ever contain it? She knew that this love was strong and deep enough to drown them both.

Celeste wept and was careful to keep her tears away from her daughter's new skin; it was bad luck to let your tears touch your children. She feared they might leave invisible scars.

"I love you, Mem," she whispered, and she kissed her daughter and the rain fell harder and she tasted Mem's salt until she knew it by heart.

Celeste without her daughter.

She will be nothing without her daughter but this doesn't frighten her anymore. She would like to be nothing. Mem must never know. She breathes in but it's harder now, everything is so heavy, the air in her lungs is cumbersome. The door in front of her is huge and weighs a thousand pounds. All she knows is that she loves her daughter. It is all she knew the day Mem was born, the day of her First Funeral, the day with the old man. It is all she has ever known. She loves her daughter.

She loves her daughter.

She opens the door.

ACKNOWLEDGMENTS

My Literary Advocates

My agent and crusader, Marianne Merola, from Brandt & Hochman
Literary Agents, Inc., for years of laser-sharp reading, guidance and
loving representation through about a dozen versions of the manuscript,
for not giving up, for consistently going above and beyond.

Kate Nitze, my editor at MacAdam/Cage Publishing, for warmly helping to dead-head words and hone the narrative with devotion and a true
delight for literature.

My Family

My parents, Mona & Carl Werbock, for making me, for playing music,
telling stories, teaching me how to live every aspect of life like an art
project, for buying that big, blank book and helping me to fill it with my
own stories, for my first typewriter (the green Olivetti manual), for my
first computer, for a lifetime of love.

My brother, Sage Werbock, for fearlessly diving into the creative process
and understanding the drive to make something out of nothing.

My in-laws, Louise D'Alessandro & Rick Hamilton, for being early
readers, for getting us the printer and providing unconditional support,
Bob O'Donnell & Donna Gentile-O'Donnell, for helping me develop
my shabby storytelling techniques and always being willing to celebrate
even the smallest of victories with homemade soup and great wine.

My uncle Alfred Paul & Aunt Sharon Paul, for all of the love and
incredible food.

My uncle Jeff Werbock, one of the first readers, for all of the enthusiasm. Cousins Ian and Peter O'Donnell for all of your affection, good humor and style.

My Teachers

Susan Field, my first-grade Language Arts teacher, who pushed me to enter the Young Authors' Contest and convinced me that I would some-day see my name on the spine of a book.

Robin Youngren, my 6th-grade English teacher, who secretly submitted one of my poems to a literary magazine and jumped up and down in the middle of the hall with me when it was accepted for publication.

Heather Ody, my 8th-grade English teacher, for decades of confidence.

Dr. Richard Wertime, English professor at Arcadia University, for bol-stering my confidence and forcing me to apply to the University of East Anglia.

Professor David Bassuk, without whom I would never have graduated.

John Scanlon, editor at The Northeast Times, aka Chief, for giving a green rookie the opportunity of a lifetime, teaching me everything I know about journalism, and always cheerleading my creative writing efforts, even when they took me away from the paper.

Jim Burtt, high-school Humanities teacher and lifetime friend, for decades of love, brutal honesty, and faith.

My Mental Health Mentors

Marylin Amidon, without whom I have no doubt I would not be here today, for your love, for your very patient guidance, intelligence and wicked sense of humor.

Rick Rappaport, guru extraordinaire, for helping me to move my own narrative point of view from the first to the third person, for keeping me present, for being the change.

My Employers (who made sure I could write and still pay my bills)
Janine Daniels, for getting me my first teaching grant.
Kelly Green at the Institute for the Study of Civic Values, for years of
wonderful opportunities.
Elise Schiller at the National School and Community Corps. &
EducationWorks.
Ignatius Weekes and Julia C. Weekes at NANA, Inc. & Grow From
Your Roots, who kept me working no matter what, for teaching me how
to charge what I'm worth.
John Taaffe at Carson Valley School.

My Friends & Chosen Family
Sheri Elfman, Matthew Hollerbush, Marielle Mariano, Alfredo & Rayne
Matthews, Holly Pester, Dave & Philippa Stasuik, Kira Strong, Dylan &
Ella Walker, for being there to share celebrations and laments.
My students, for providing constant inspiration and keeping me present.
Julia C. Weekes, my best friend and sister, my most valuable reader, this
book could not, would not, have become what it is without you.
My husband, Casey O'Donnell, for all of the chocolate croissants, for
living with me through this whole process, for never telling me to give
up and get a real job, for always supporting this bizarre idea I had of pur-
suing a lifelong dream of becoming an author and having a family.
My son, Kieran O'Donnell, for arriving this year and making the other
half of that dream come true.

Suggested Discussion Questions for Reading Groups

1. Why do you think the author selected Open Me as the title for this book? What does it mean for Mem or any other character to be "opened?" What are they encouraged to expose or taught to keep hidden?

2. The "historical" pieces sandwiched between each chapter are artifacts O'Donnell created to help reveal the history of Wailers from around the world. As faux excerpts of praise and blame, these relics were designed to serve as documentation that does not really exist. Why do you think there is so little real documentation available about Wailers? What is the cost of being feared and revered throughout the ages?

3. O'Donnell was a poet for many years before writing Open Me. In what ways is her training as a poet evident throughout the book? How does this poetic influence shape the narrative? Do you think it helps or hinders the storytelling?

4. Why do you think Mem remains loyal to her mother even after she has been abused and exploited? How does Mem's mother use shame and guilt as tools to reinforce this generational dynamic? What role do the Lessons play in maintaining this mother-daughter legacy?

5. Mem has been raised to understand that everything (and everyone) in this world is temporary, that all living creatures die and all material objects will eventually disintegrate or turn into something else. What are the benefits of possessing this kind of understanding at such a young age? What is the cost?

6. What does Mem fear most? What does Mem's mother fear most? How are these fears interdependent?

7. Each chapter in the book begins with a question. Who do you think is asking these questions? Are the questions themselves important? Do the questions ever get answered?

8. Mem often has a voice in her head that offers a cruel running commentary. How does this voice change as Mem grows older? How did it get there? What purpose does it serve? What do you think Mem will have to do as an adult to control the voice?

9. Why do you think that, historically, mourning has been the role of women? Why do you think there are so few male characters in the story?

10. What is the significance of the Wailers having private and public names? How are the ideas of "public" and "private" defined and emphasized for Mem?

11. Even though she grows up in a typical suburban town, Mem spends most of her life feeling like an outsider. Sometimes this sense of being different from others is a point of pride and sometimes it becomes cause for suffering. How are these beliefs fortified by her mother? By the rest of society?

12. One of the first things O'Donnell realized when she began writing this book was that she would be a terrible Wailer because she hates crying in public. Do you think you could be a good Wailer? If you so, what would be your specialty?